Tropical Encounter

Tropical Breeze Series Book One

Michele Gilcrest

Get A FREE Ebook!

Would you like a FREE ebook? JOIN Michele's newsletter to receive information about new releases, giveaways, and special promotions! To say thank you, I'll send you a FREE copy of The Inn at Pelican Beach. Sign up today!

https://dl.bookfunnel.com/wr9wvokoin

Chapter 1

Meg

Meg Carter gazed at the wedding cake assortment displayed on the table. She and her fiancée, John, tested several pieces when it finally hit her. They were getting nowhere with making a decision about the cake, wedding favors, or anything for that matter, and the wedding was less than sixty days away.

Surrounded by the Ritz Carlton-like glam of Manhattan with wait staff at one's beck and call was more his thing. But she went along with it, holding her own, being well groomed by working in the hotel industry.

"I'm so confused," Meg moaned, seeking direction from the wedding planner.

Trish winked at her. "It's not your fault. They're all delicious. Besides, being undecided is completely normal. How about you two cleanse your palate with a glass of water and talk it over. There's no rush. Take all the time you need."

Once Trish left, Meg laid her fork down and slid her hand over John's. "I'm sorry, babe. I imagined this being a lot easier.

Honestly, I feel like we should just go with the chocolate cake and call it a day. Anything to get past all the decision making, and just be done with it."

John loosened his tie completely and backed away from the table. "I disagree."

Meg slumped in her chair, staring beyond him to the streetlights of midtown Manhattan. Although accustomed to the hustle and bustle of a big city, she was known for her easy-going personality, faith-filled and lighthearted temperament. She had a New York edge to her when the situation called for it. But overall, she was patient and supportive. Relationship-wise, she'd remained by John's side, stretching their engagement out for three years, while his travel for work came first. She waited so long to be married, mainly due to never quite finding the right one until now. Most importantly, she loved him, and sometimes that's the kind of sacrifice one made for love. At least, she thought it was.

Meg perked up, nudging him on the arm. "You can decide. I don't care what we have for dessert. The most important thing to me is that we're finally getting married, John. Cake or no cake, that's what matters most, right?"

He glanced at his polished shoes. "That's the part I'm struggling with, Meg. This is such a huge deal. We shouldn't want to carelessly rush past all the decision making, just so we can get on with the wedding. How we make decisions today is an indicator of how we'll make decisions for the rest of our lives together. That's rather important, don't you think?"

"Of course, but, in the grand scheme of things, it's just cake," she mumbled.

"I'm just calling it like I see it. I think our problems stretch far beyond sampling wedding cake and altering the guest list. We're not on the same page about anything, Meg."

"That's not fair. I've always been supportive of you even when we didn't see eye-to-eye. We've successfully made plenty of decisions in the past. It's almost as if you're looking for a problem. I just think you're tired. Maybe we should put this off until the weekend. "Meg folded the napkin on her lap and gathered her purse.

"I'm seeing someone else," he said, fumbling over his words while clearing his throat.

She knew she heard his voice audibly uttering something, but surely he didn't say those words. Anything but those dreaded words.

"What did you say?"

Again, sounding as if something was stuck in his throat, he repeated, "I said, I'm seeing someone else."

Stunned at the audacity and nerve, she froze. "I see. You didn't think to mention this before now? "Meg clenched hard enough to feel her nails digging into her skin. She noticed as John got up and paced near the window. Probably a safe move on his part. She wasn't violent, but her blood was boiling in the most unusual way.

"I've been trying to find a way to bring it up. A couple of weeks ago I even went as far as thinking maybe I should break it off," he explained.

"Uh, ya think?"

"Hear me out, Meg. At the end of the day, it all comes back to one thing. We're disconnected, and we have been for a very long time. We're not the same people we were when we first met. We both want different things out of life."

Still stunned, she said, "Interesting... who is she?"

"It doesn't matter. Look, you're a great woman, Meg. I know someday you're going to make some lucky guy very happy —"

She tilted her head, still in total disbelief as John continued to talk.

"You've always lived your life according to good values and principles, and I admire you for that. I just don't know that I want a family, or a nice house and a white picket fence. The typical American dream may not be for me anymore."

Meg's mouth dropped open. "You said you wanted all of those things when we first met. Has our whole relationship been one big lie?"

He walked over to her chair and took her by the hands. "No. It hasn't been. I'd be a fool to sit here and try to blame all of this on you. I'm the one who's changed, not you. Sadly, I picked a really bad time to tell you. I don't know what I want out of life anymore. I question so many things, including whether or not I want to stay in my career field, whether I ever want kids. I feel like I don't even know who I am anymore."

She removed her hands from his and lowered her voice.

"John, after all these years, the least you could've done was be upfront with me. We could've figured this out. Now I'm supposed to sit here and believe it was some sort of pre-mid-life crisis that led you to another woman? Please! Give me a break."

Just then, Trish entered the room holding another tray. "I think I have a solution you're both going to love," she said, with a grin that quickly dissipated once she saw their faces.

Meg stood up, keeping her eyes locked on John's the entire time. "Trish... John and I would like to thank you for your time and hard work. Unfortunately, the wedding is being called off. As it turns out, deciding which cake we want on our wedding day was the least of our problems. Maintaining a monogamous and trustworthy relationship is the far greater issue here, isn't that right, John?"

He held his head down and didn't respond.

"Exactly," she grunted.

Then, she glanced down at the three-carat ring he once proudly presented to her. She was sure the cost was peanuts to him in comparison to what he was worth. He was born and bred in a family of financial bigwigs with silver spoons handed down through the generations. The ring probably didn't even begin to put a dent in his bank account when he bought it. Either way, since it was hers, she'd find a way to put it to good use, because giving it back wouldn't be an option.

"I could stand here and go on about how wrong you are for this. But it would be a waste of time. Just see to it that you cover all costs associated with canceling the wedding. And— see to it that you never dial my number again."

With a hair toss, Meg swung around, catching a glimpse of a pitcher filled with water. She knew it wasn't right, but she was overcome with the urge to pick it up and submerge him, the same way he haphazardly submerged her with grief.

Before she could think straight, the deed had been done. John's hands were outstretched as he looked down at his clothes that were dripping wet. As he stood with his mouth wide open, she confidently dug her heels into the plush carpet and exited the room.

Six weeks later, Meg handed over her last box as the moving company loaded all of her belongings. She went through the motions of checking the closets and kitchen drawers to make sure nothing was left behind, when her girlfriend, Casey, of thirty-five years tapped on the partially opened apartment door.

"Knock, knock."

"Hey, Case, come on in."

She peered around. "Would you look at this place? Gosh, before now I thought there was a chance you might change your mind. But somehow this move just got real. I don't think I'm ready for this, Meg."

Meg slid her hands into her jean pockets. "Oh, it's real alright. My things are all packed up, and I made arrangements to rent a beach house for the first year. You know, just to try something new and exciting. Oh, and I start my new job at the first of the month. If that isn't real, then I don't know what is."

Casey reached out and embraced Meg with her arms opened wide. "Meg Carter, you are one in a million. What on earth am I going to do without my best friend?"

Meg squeezed her tight, then stood back, gripping her by the shoulders. "Don't worry. You're not getting rid of me that easily. I'm going to need somebody to help knock some sense into me when I get weak and think about coming back to New York."

"True, but I doubt you'll do that. You may need time to adjust, but working in the hotel industry, whether abroad or on some tropical island, has been your dream since you were a teenager. Think about it, prior to meeting John, you applied for a similar position. This is your chance to make a life-long dream come true."

Meg offered a folding chair to Casey. It was left for her when she took over the studio apartment, so she figured she'd pay it forward, leaving it for the renters to come.

"You're right. I was such a fool to delay my dreams for him. Here I am almost four years later, starting over from scratch."

"I beg to differ. You are a five-time award winning Director of Sales, and a darn good one, might I add. It's your experience here in New York that helped you to land that job, so I wouldn't make light of it."

Meg smiled, leaning back on the breakfast counter. "I can't deny my blessings. But I also can't help but think how much happier I'd be if I had never met John. Sometimes I replay our last conversation over and over in my mind, but no matter how many times I do, I just can't make sense of what he did to me."

"You never will. You are so much better than him, Meg. I'm just thankful he finally showed his true colors before you said I do."

"True," Meg agreed, wandering over to the big window that overlooked the city.

Casey stood beside her, gazing in the same direction. "God knows I don't want to see you go. But, somehow, I have a feeling this is going to be the best thing that's ever happened to you."

Meg sighed. "Just in case, will you save your spare room for me?" She giggled.

"My guest room will always have your name on it. But you better save a spare room for me in that rental of yours. A whole beach house to yourself for a year! Let me guess, you cashed in that ring of yours, didn't you?"

Meg winked. "Now, does that sound like something I would do?"

The room fell silent for a minute before they both burst into laughter.

When the laughter settled, the distinct sound of children playing in the apartment above caught their attention.

Meg closed her eyes and pointed upward. "Now that is something I won't miss. I love this city, but from now on, I want to hear nothing but the peace and tranquility of the beach. That's it, nothing else."

"Oh, Meg. Take me with you."

"I wouldn't dare. My sweet goddaughters need their mother, and Craig needs his wife. But, don't you worry. I'll travel back every once in a while, to check on my dad and my stepmother. During my visits, we'll make it our business to get together and play catch up."

Casey extended her hand. "It's a deal." Then she paused. "Speaking of your dad, how did he take the news about you moving to the Bahamas?"

"After he got over the initial urge to kick John's you know what — he made me reassure him this was something I really wanted for myself. Then, he gave me his blessing."

Meg faced her dear friend. "I realize how much of a big deal it is, making the decision to pack up your whole life and start something new. Especially something so far away from home. I'll admit, at first it was all about me running away from the life I knew with John. I wanted to get as far away from him as I could. But, not now, Case. It's different. I'm getting back to the core of who I am, my dreams, and how I was led to live my life from the very beginning. I want to be the best lead sales director the hotel industry has to offer. And —" she hesitated, "maybe someday, I can take my dreams even further and open up my own resort. Who knows?"

"Sweetheart, if that passion is stirring up on the inside of you, the only thing that's left to do is go and chase after those dreams with all your might. Just know that you have a family that's supporting you. Even if it's from afar. Oh, and one last thing," Casey said.

"What's that?"

"You may be hurting right now, but be sure to leave room in your heart to meet somebody new. Promise me you will?" she asked.

"Mm, now you're pushing your luck. I'll settle for grabbing something to eat before Dad arrives to take me to the airport."

Casey put her arm around Meg's shoulders as they walked out of the apartment together. "Okay, so maybe we can approach this with baby steps. First you unpack and get settled, then —"

"Caseyyyy, quit while you're ahead. I'm done with the

dating scene. Period. If I'm ever to be married again, he'd literally have to fall from the sky and land on my front doorstep. And, since that's not likely to happen, I think we can leave the whole idea alone," Meg emphasized with confidence.

"Mm hmm. We'll see."

Chapter 2

Meg

Meg scrambled with one hand, digging inside her purse to give the cab driver a tip while finagling her cell in the other hand. With a three-hour flight behind her, she'd finally stepped foot on Bahamian soil, standing just a few feet away from her beach house rental.

"Yes, Dad. I just arrived at the house and I'm fine. The flight was wonderful, my taxi driver knew exactly where to take me, and from what I can tell, the place looks pretty good."

She passed along the tip and mouthed "thank you" to the driver, then proceeded to walk up a pathway towing her luggage behind her. A few weeds and overgrown plants caught her attention, but it was nothing she couldn't fix.

"Dad, please don't worry about me. I promise to check in with you again tomorrow as soon as I get settled in."

She stopped, allowing her gaze to scan across the coral shiplap with dingy white trim. The place looked like it hadn't been occupied. In fact, it looked very different from the way it was advertised online.

A bit dusty, but still livable, she thought to herself. A slightly different version of what she just told her father.

"What was that, Dad?" she asked.

"I'm checking under the front mat now, and, yes... the key is here, as expected. Okay, I have to go now, but I promise, promise, promise to call you in the morning. I love you, Dad."

After disconnecting the call, Meg noticed cobwebs connecting from one end of the front porch to the other. Not exactly a good sign of what was to come. Online, the property management company received five stars, with several comments, giving accolades for their vacation rental accommodations. Therefore, her first thought was "what happened to this place?" A question she'd seek the answer to once she gave them a call in the morning.

Inside, Meg stood in the foyer, observing the open-floor concept and the furniture draped in sheets. The dark and deserted look wasn't exactly what she had in mind for a beach house retreat, but with a little TLC, it would do.

Out of curiosity, Meg placed her bags down and removed one of the sheets. "Wicker furniture in the living room... okay. Not my first choice," she said.

She then opened the shutters, letting in what was left of the remaining daylight.

After locating the bedrooms with more furniture draped in dingy sheets, the bathrooms, and touring the kitchen, she discovered a back door, leading to the main attraction. Finally, she found what she was looking for... the beach...the tranquility of the waves... her happy place resting several feet beyond a pool. There wasn't much left to discover after this.

Meg closed her eyelids and listened, allowing herself to be immersed by the sound.

Exhaling, she said out loud, "I wasn't expecting dated appliances and cobwebs in every corner of the house, but this...

this is what I call living. If this doesn't make up for the chaos I left behind in New York, I don't know what will."

The sound of a man's deep voice clearing his throat startled her.

"Ma'am, I believe what you're doing is called trespassing."

Meg jumped, to the point of nearly knocking an empty planter over.

"Oh my gosh. Who are you?" she asked, grabbing a nearby sundial as if she could use it as a weapon.

The strange man looked at Meg, then at the sundial, then back at Meg.

"Shouldn't I be the one concerned about protecting myself? After all, this is my property."

She watched as he dangled a key in his hand. Noticing the key had the same orange ring as the one she'd found under the mat, she relaxed slightly.

"So, you must be my landlord. It's nice to meet you. I would assume you're here to officially welcome me, although I must say, there has to be some sort of rule about bursting in on your tenants," She snarled.

Meg watched as his facial expression shifted from curious to almost clueless.

"Now that you're here, perhaps we can have a conversation about your false advertising. The website clearly showed a fully furnished beach house with beautiful white furniture, and it was free from all the cobwebs. This place looks as if it hasn't been occupied in God knows how long. Oh, and what's with all the outdoor wicker furniture? I mean, it's not terrible, but again, it looks nothing like what I saw online. And wicker in every single room is overkill, don't you think?"

He stepped forward, which made her cautiously take a step back.

"I'm sorry. There has to be some sort of mix-up. I'm not

sure how you found this place, or how you even got in. But, I'm the new owner, Parker Wilson. This was a bank-owned property that I purchased at an auction. The bank never said a word to me about having a tenant."

Meg took an additional step back, then leaned on the banister overlooking the pool and the long stretch of beach. "No. Eh eh, that can't be right. I have proof. I have paperwork that shows I paid my rent up to a year in advance for this beach house. The address on the form is 495 South Coral Lane, right here on Providence Island. I'll go get the papers right now and show you."

She stormed past him, returning inside to search in her purse.

Cautiously following her in, he continued, "Ma'am, I don't doubt that you believe you're supposed to be here. But I believe my deed trumps any paperwork that you received online. You might want to start by calling the company who collected rent from you. I'm sure they have an explanation for this."

By this point Meg turned around, flashing the papers at him, practically shoving them in his hand. "See, here's the confirmation right here. I even followed the instructions to get the keys from under the mat. That's how I got inside, therefore not trespassing, but fully possessing the right to be here."

Noticing her hand was still forcing the papers in his, she backed off a bit. She observed his business suit, his hair that was neatly combed, and the scent of his cologne which was ever-so subtle, yet intoxicating, in a good way.

He's probably a city slicker, trying to get over, she thought. Knowing that even several miles away from the big apple, city slickers still existed.

"What was your name again?" she asked.

"Parker," he replied, reading over her documents and

scratching his head. He pulled out his cell phone and started sliding up and down on the screen.

"What are you doing?"

He looked up. "Well, for one, I'm trying to see if this company is legit. How did you find out about them, anyway? Are you from around here?"

Meg drew in a deep breath and let it out again, trying to settle her head from spinning, and still trying to decide if she should even trust him.

"Where I'm from is irrelevant. Let's just say, I did a little research, read the reviews, and since others spoke very highly of the company, I decided to take a leap of faith."

She waved her hand around the room. "Now, clearly, they weren't one-hundred percent honest about the conditions, but it's not that bad. I'll have to do a little work before my things are delivered, but I can make it work."

His eyebrows scrunched together. "Whoa. You're having your belongings delivered to this address?"

"Duh. Of course, I am. I need the rest of my clothes, shoes, and other personal items in order to start my new job on Monday. Again, enough with all the questions about me. What are your search results showing about the company?"

He continued to scroll before giving up. "I'm not getting anything. It's probably worth it to make a phone call in the morning and do a little digging around. In the meantime, we have ourselves a bit of a problem. My contractors are waiting on standby to begin demo next week. Plus, I'm staying here while the work is being done. As in, moving in tonight. I'm not sure what your plans are, but you'll need to find other accommodations."

"Excuse me? I can't leave. As mentioned earlier, I paid one full year's worth of rent to be here. One... full... year. Do you know how many thousands of dollars that is? And, who does that? Living on site while flipping a house? That doesn't make any sense. Sounds kind of fishy, if you ask me."

She watched as Parker looked at her luggage and then paced several steps before leaning on the counter.

"What sounds fishy is your rental agreement. And, not that I have to explain myself, but I'm not a traditional investor. I intentionally choose properties that I want to renovate room by room, while living in it. This helps me to cut down on expenses. I do it for about six months to a year, and then I move on."

As he spoke, she noticed a sense of warmth in his eyes mixed with the weariness of someone who'd worked hard all day. Perhaps that would explain the business attire. What she hadn't seen yet was proof that he actually belonged there. "I see. Well, if you're really on the up and up, it might be nice if you would start by providing some tangible proof. Who's to say I shouldn't be dialing 911 as we speak?"

Parker surrendered with a smirk on his face. "Fair enough. It just so happens that my mother raised me to be a gentleman. Therefore, as much as I was hoping to immediately settle in and prepare for an important meeting in the morning, I will humor you and go get my deed."

As he pulled open the front door, Meg opened her mouth to say something else but thought better of it. She was slowly coming to the realization that she may be in a predicament, which made her stomach feel sick. Just over a month ago, anger led her to cash in her engagement ring, giving some of the proceeds to charity, and almost all the rest to put toward renting the beach house. Any additional funds she had was for emergency savings. She'd sworn not to touch her account on a whim, and she certainly wasn't prepared to explain any of this to her dad. Not after flying there to make her dreams a reality. No way. It wasn't happening.

Parker returned with a couple of documents and his license in hand. "Here's all the proof you could possibly need. The deed shows that I have the right address, and here's my license to prove that I am who I say I am."

She skimmed over his license, reading his name, the words 'government of the commonwealth of the Bahamas', and paid particular attention to his license number. She also noticed his DOB, making him forty years old, a year older than she was.

A rush of nausea rose in her stomach, along with tears and an overwhelming sense of not knowing what to do. "This has to be some sort of mistake," she said, holding back the flood gates from letting loose. "I mean, I thought I did a good job at vetting the company."

Parker reached out, awkwardly trying to console her, and then retreated his hand, running it through the side of his hair instead.

"Ma'am, did you check with the Better Business Bureau? These days it's not uncommon for scammers to set up fake reviews on websites. It's just another crafty way to lure in their prey."

She shook her head. "I didn't think that far ahead. I had a lot going on with my virtual job interviews, and —"

Meg fell silent, leaving Parker scrambling to figure things out.

"I guess that's all hindsight," He sighed. "Look, do you have any family or friends in the area? I'd normally offer to call a few hotels for you, but there's an annual convention in town known for overbooking the local hotels for at least two weeks."

Her eyes were still filled with tears as she tried to think logically about the next step. "I can't leave."

"I'm sorry?"

She wiped her face and took somewhat of a stronger stance. "I'm not from the area and I have nowhere else to go. Plus, I haven't even had a chance to speak to the leasing company yet. Somebody over there owes me an explanation. One would think they were the owners before you bought the place, right?"

"I doubt it. But, even if that were the case, according to the bank, they didn't pay their bills, therefore sending this house into foreclosure and forfeiting their rights."

Meg stood speechless, feeling the evening breeze from the back door brush against her neck. If there was ever a time she needed a sign to guide her, this was it.

There was always the option of returning to Nassau's International airport, catching the first flight back home. But there was no place to call home. Her girlfriend's guest room wasn't a long-term plan. And, her dad, heaven knows he loved her dearly, but he was a newlywed, given a fresh start with someone new after years of being alone. Her mother passed when she was a young girl, and she didn't have the heart to interrupt his new marriage. Just like she didn't have the heart to give up her new job or reverse all of her plans. She'd already made it this far and had to figure something out.

"I'm assuming you already toured the house?" Parker asked, not even making eye contact at this point.

Meg waved her hand around as if showcasing the place. "Just a quick walk-through to see the layout."

He raised his eyebrows. "Mm. Well, I don't have the heart to kick a lady to the curb. Although, I have to tell you, I'm stepping out on a limb here, trusting that you're sane and won't cause me any trouble," He said.

"Me? No, I wouldn't dare cause any trouble. I just need until the morning to give the company a call, and if that doesn't work, call around and see if anyone is renting a room. I didn't plan on incurring any additional expenses until I'd been on the job for a while."

Parker nodded. "Mm hmm. Well, for tonight, the least I can

do is offer you to take the master bedroom with the en-suite. That way you'll have your privacy. I can stay in the loft upstairs and use the guest bathroom, assuming that it's actually functioning."

"There's a loft upstairs? I don't recall seeing that online."

She followed Parker with her eyes, watching as he removed his suit jacket while opening the refrigerator. Seeming somewhat displeased at the sight, he closed the door.

"Ma'am —"

She interrupted, "Please call me Meg... Meg Carter."

"Miss Carter, it's very possible that what you saw online was a false ad just so they could swindle you out of your money."

The comment stung. Standing several feet away from this very tall and handsome stranger, he may not have known much about her, but he had one thing right. She'd been naive. Who would do such a thing? Who would actually charge all that money online, being so trusting without at least investigating to make sure the company could deliver? She rested her hand on her hip. "I'd still like to think there's a simple explanation for this."

In order to keep from staring, she diverted her attention toward the living room.

"I realize some things don't add up. For example, why are there sheets everywhere covering all the furniture? It's certainly not how the place was displayed online. Did the bank have an explanation for that?"

"They did. According to them, this was a vacation property originally owned by a woman who left it to her grandkids. Unfortunately, being young, they didn't have the means to occupy the place and take care of it properly, so it went into foreclosure. When you were speaking earlier, I didn't want to burst your bubble, but I highly doubt her grandkids would've been your landlord."

Again, Meg pushed out a long breath and closed her eyes. "I'm such an idiot. At this rate, I highly doubt I'll see any of that money again."

"Don't be so hard on yourself. This kind of thing happens to people all the time," he said.

She interlocked her fingers together, trying to brainstorm, but came up with absolutely nothing. "Not people like me. I'm usually on my A-game, highly in tune and aware of what's going on. If the last couple of months of my life hadn't been such a big distraction, I highly doubt I'd be in this mess."

"Dare I ask?" he said with a gentle smile.

"It's not worth talking about."

She fell silent, catching a glimpse of the palm trees swaying more aggressively than when she'd arrived. She realized she hadn't eaten, she hadn't unpacked her bags, and she was in for a long night with Parker, who was practically a stranger.

Chapter 3

Parker

Parker Wilson peered out the front shutters, waiting for pizza to be delivered. It had already been a doozy of a day, signing pages upon pages at his closing. Immediately following, he made phone calls, lined up estimates and contractors, and he'd even taken another look at his budget, tweaking a few things as needed.

After that, Parker was counting on a quiet night. Sure, he anticipated an adjustment period as he spent the first night in a new space. But a gorgeous woman staying under the same roof? That hadn't been in the cards for the evening, and he still wasn't sure it was a wise idea.

"I hope you don't mind, but I ordered a large pizza pie, half with everything, and the other half plain," He explained.

"You could've ordered a horse and I would've been thrilled. Anything goes when you're starving. Besides, I really like pizza just about any way you slice it. Here, allow me to contribute. How much was the bill, again?" Meg asked, reaching for her purse.

He waved at her, dismissing the suggestion. "I have it covered."

Parker rolled up his sleeves and began carefully removing some of the dusty sheets from the furniture, at times sneezing as he maneuvered. "Looks like I have my work cut out for me. This place doesn't look as if it's been touched in a couple of years."

He noticed Meg looking around, taking it all in. There was something about her that was intriguing. Perhaps it was her not-so-subtle gestures, or the blond highlights in her hair. Or the fact that she reminded him of his deceased wife who'd died two years earlier.

She smiled, looking around her. "Yes, but with some elbow grease and a few updates it will be an absolute gem. The direct access to the beach makes this place so inviting. It's probably worth a pretty penny, I'll bet. I certainly paid top dollar to rent here, that's for sure."

Parker tried not to stare as she flipped her curls over her shoulder and began helping him remove another sheet. "If you don't mind me asking, what led you to rent a big house like this all by yourself?"

Her eyebrows raised. "Without getting into the weeds, I needed a fresh start. It's that simple."

Parker paused, giving her a half smile. "Nothing is that simple. We all need to hit the reset button every now and again, but that doesn't necessarily equate to renting a sprawling beach house online, presumably from out of state."

"You have me there. But, unlike others, I've always had a dream of advancing my career in hospitality to include working at a resort. It's the reason I moved here." She hesitated then continued. "The beach house was a reward to myself. Maybe even a reward mixed with a little revenge, I don't know. At the end of the day, I needed to do something to kick my lifelong dream off to a good start. Renting this place was supposed to be a gift to myself. Eventually, I knew I would have to give up the beach house, and settle in somewhere more practical, but opportunities like this don't come around very often, so I wanted to take advantage, if you will. I mean, who wouldn't enjoy one year of relaxing and clearing your mind while taking in this pretty view?"

Parker continued listening while poking around in a few nearby closets for something to dust with. When he returned, she had placed her hair in a bun, revealing hoop earrings that decorated the side of her neck just so. He had to remind himself to stay focused.

"Whoever he is, he must've done a real number on you!" He chuckled.

"Excuse me?"

"You heard me. Whoever it was that broke your heart must've done a real number on you. That's the only reason a woman would ever describe her beach rental as a gift and revenge all in the same breath."

He could tell he hit a nerve by the bulge on her left temple. It didn't seem to be as pronounced until he opened his mouth and inserted foot. Next time he'd think better of it. At least, he'd try. Being frank came like second nature to him. Although, she definitely seemed like she could hold her own with a quick comeback if she wanted to.

Meg proceeded to step closer as if she were going to tell him a thing or two, but the headlights from a car stopped her in her tracks.

Parker held his finger up. "Hold that thought."

"Mm hmm."

Outside, he slipped the delivery guy a bill, asking him to keep the change. The hot box gave off an aroma, triggering his stomach to an undeniable growl. The pizza coupled with a soda would hit the spot, giving him the fuel needed to prep for his meeting in the morning.

Back inside, Meg was clearing a table, making the glass top shine again. It was amazing how a little glass cleaner and the touch of a woman could bring a place back to life again.

"One large pizza pie coming right up," he sang melodiously, placing the box on the table.

He then pointed across the room. "There's another roll of paper towels on the counter if you want to pull off a sheet and use it as a plate."

"Thanks," she said.

Parker grabbed a slice and consumed a large bite, followed by a long moan. When he opened his eyes, she was staring right at him with one eyebrow raised higher than the other.

With a full mouth he explained. "Mm, sorry. I haven't eaten all day."

She gave him a half-hearted smile. "Please, don't mind me. I think I'm going to just take a couple of slices and head back to my room. That way you can eat in peace."

Parker popped open the lid to his soda can. Even if it was only for one night, how could they coexist in the same house without at least getting to know something about the other?

"Why don't you pull up a chair and at least hang around for dinner? I don't know that a bedroom covered in old sheets is the most appealing place to eat your food."

Shrugging her shoulders, Meg shifted gears and pulled out a chair before picking out her first slice. He watched as she sat down, bowing her head for what seemed like a full minute, then proceeded to dig in.

He took a swig, then spoke up. "In all fairness, I wasn't really expecting this... the whole idea of having a roomie for the night. I'm sure you weren't either."

Meg quickly corrected him. "We're not roomies, just housemates for the evening until I get to the bottom of things."

Nodding his head up and down in agreement, Parker continued. "About that. What are you expecting will come of this? I've already proven to you that I own the house."

She held up her finger to swallow her food, then spoke. "Yes, but, what if there's a mix-up? An unexplained mix-up that will only make sense once I talk to a manager?"

Parker's eyes drifted down to his pizza as he tried to find the right words. He didn't want to be rude, but mix-up or not, it wouldn't change the fact that he was the owner, and he was continuing forward with his plans for renovation. Plain and simple. So, if she wanted to be in denial, or needed to wait to hear some official tell her how badly she got duped out of her money, that was on her.

He continued. "Right. Sooo... back to the guy we were talking about earlier. The one who did you wrong," he replied.

"You know what? You have a lot of nerve! Are you always this forward with people you don't know?"

He nearly wanted to kick himself for what he was about to say next, but his flesh had already gotten the best of him, and he could already feel the words rolling off his tongue. His eyes took a sharp turn her way while taking another bite of his pizza. "Forward? Why? For stating the truth? I noticed you haven't denied it. And, I guess you'll have to forgive me in advance, but I don't know you from Adam. So, before we both go to bed tonight, in separate bedrooms, yet under the same roof, one would think you'd like to share some surface level information and vice versa. The only reason why I made a comment about the guy is you seemed awfully testy when you mentioned the word revenge."

A look of seriousness washed over her like a wave at the shore. Then, just as quickly the look washed away, she busted into laughter, lessening the tension in the room. Meg drew a long piece of cheese from the slice to her mouth, then smiled. "I did say it with a little zing, didn't I? It probably sounded like I had some sort of chip on my shoulder," she laughed.

"Uh, yeahhh. Just a little testy. From the sound of things, you may have come here for your career, but you're also running away from something. Or someone."

She sipped her soda while glaring at him. "Who are you supposed to be? Some sort of mind reader, or perhaps even a therapist?"

"Neither. I just recognize the voice of a woman who's been through a thing or two."

A slow smile raised on the corner of her mouth. "Oh, really, now? What about you? What's your story? What's a forty-year-old guy like yourself doing moving around from house to house without a wife and kids? Surely there's a story just waiting to be revealed," she nudged.

He noticed how observant she was, obviously picking up on his age when he showed her his license. If he had to guess, Parker figured he was the older of the two, but he couldn't tell by how many years.

After devouring the last bite, he reached for another slice. "Of course, everyone has a story to tell, but in this case, like yourself, I plead the fifth. Instead, I'd rather start with something simple, like where I'm from."

He noticed as Meg's eyes bulged at the double standard, but she listened just the same.

"My full name is Parker Wilson, and as you mentioned, I'm forty years old. Good catch, by the way. I would imagine you picked that up from my license. I'm originally from Chicago, Illinois, and I've been living here for almost four years while focusing on my real estate business."

"Hmm, Chicago. The Windy City. What brought you all the way to the Bahamas from Chicago?" she asked.

"Family. I have a sister back in Chicago, and a sister who lives here and is married with two kids. Her husband had to relocate out here because of his job, and let's just say — after visiting back and forth, I fell in love with the idea of living a new life along the Bahamian shores. Eventually, I decided to make it my home."

Meg melted comfortably into her seat. "That makes sense. You and your sister must be pretty close."

"We are. Sometimes we find ourselves at odds over little things, but nothing important enough to come between us. Plus, I'm pretty tight with my little niece and nephews."

As they spoke, he noticed even her smile felt comforting. That in itself was strange given that he'd never met the woman prior to today. "What about you? Any siblings?"

"No. Just a close friend who's always been like a sister. And family members who are checking on me daily. Just putting that out there in case you get any crazy ideas," she replied.

Parker allowed a long sigh to ease out in the form of a hiss. Placing his slice down, he then tilted his head and proceeded to make things clear to her.

"I shouldn't have to reiterate this, but you're the one making the decision to stay here of your own free will. Nobody's forcing you. In addition, I'm not in the business of running a hotel service. I'm doing you a favor."

She grunted, which gave him pause. Perhaps he was getting in over his head. He knew if something like this had happened to one of his sisters, he'd hope some kind soul would do the same for them. His parents raised him better than to slam the door in the face of someone who was in need. But this gal was testing the waters.

He surrendered, easing up, knowing that she probably was

just as uncomfortable as he was. "Look, I get it. You found yourself in a very inconvenient situation. One, if you had your way, would've worked out very differently. As for me, I've been told I can be a little rough around the edges at times, saying exactly what's on my mind, without thinking first. But, outside of that, you can ask anybody around here about me. I'm safe to be around, and I'm an upstanding man. If you do a little research, you can find out for yourself."

He closed the lid to the pizza box and grabbed a few of his things. "It's getting pretty late, and I have to prep for a meeting in the morning. I'm heading up to the loft to get some work done. If you need anything, just holler for me."

"Thanks again for the food... and the hospitality," she said.

Parker bowed his head slightly. "No problem. Have a good night." He then passed her by, but peered over his shoulder at her silhouette. She was the most beautiful woman he'd met in a very long time. A woman who managed to capture his attention, which until now, was unheard of. She was the perfect mix of just enough spice and just enough beauty, plus the woman prayed before she ate. Something he hadn't seen in a very long time. Either way, it didn't make a difference. Maybe if they'd met in another lifetime under different circumstances. But it was too late for all that now. He'd already made a personal vow never to love again.

Chapter 4

Meg

Meg's left hand rested on Parker's shoulder, while the other in the palm of his hand. She wondered how a man could send her heartbeat into such a rhythm as they slow-danced in unison. Whether it was the romantic beach, or the way they held each other closely. She was losing all sense of reality as they moved in unison to the first song of the evening, causing her pulse to race. Then it happened. He leaned in, slowly touching her lips with his, kissing her ever so softly.

Meg's dream was interrupted with a lunge in the upright position, gripping the sheets while gasping for air. After a long night of tossing and turning restlessly, all she wanted was a decent hour of sleep. Not a strange dream about kissing someone she hardly knew, on the dance floor at their wedding, no less. *Odd.*

A small opening in the curtains revealed a bright ray of sunshine peering through the dark room. If only she could shake off the dream, she knew a view of a beautiful oasis would await. One she'd probably be more enthusiastic about if she wasn't soon facing the reality of homelessness... which was probably an exaggeration, but the outlook wasn't good.

"Darn," she spewed, noticing the clock read ten a.m. Next to it was a torn sheet of paper where she'd written Parker's license number and birthday. It was etched in her brain just in case he wasn't the gentleman he described himself to be.

"Three missed calls from Dad. Great, Meg, just great."

She flung the sheet back, gathered her bearings on the edge of the bed, and cleared her throat. "Okay, just call and tell him everything is fine. Be honest about the condition of the place, and tell him you're working it out." She rehearsed, but before she could dial, there was a knock at her door.

"Just a minute," she called out.

Meg leapt toward a nearby mirror, swooshing her hair back and forth until it fell in a somewhat reasonable direction. She wiped the corner of her eyes and took a deep breath. A polka dot pajama set wasn't exactly the kind of outfit she wanted on public display, but at least she was fully covered.

She flew open the curtains, then walked over to the door, leaving a slight opening to greet him.

"Hey," he said, standing awkwardly while giving her a quick wave. She could tell he was trying his best not to look directly at her, of course, making things even more awkward.

"Hi. I'm sorry. Apparently, I overslept," she said, glancing back toward the messy room.

"Don't apologize. You probably needed the rest. I'm actually heading in town to the meeting I told you about. I should be back in a couple of hours. In the meantime, I ran to the little corner store and picked up some breakfast sandwiches, along with coffee and left everything in the kitchen. I wasn't sure what you liked, so you have a few options to choose from."

Meg revealed her dimples, graciously thanking him for the gesture. It didn't go unnoticed that he was wearing a new suit, a different colored tie, and was better looking than she'd observed the day before. Of course, that was the last thing her mind needed to focus on, so she snapped out of it.

"You didn't have to do that. I could have easily grabbed another slice of pizza leftover from last night."

"Ha, about that. I've been known to have a ferocious appetite at times. I devoured the rest of the pizza while I was prepping for my meeting. I probably need to swing by a grocery store on my way back, but in the meantime, I didn't want you to wake up starving."

"Thank you. I appreciate it. Oh, and I hope to have some answers for you by the time you return. I plan on breaking out the laptop and doing some research first thing," she explained.

"Yeah, good luck with that. I was able to work offline last night, but the cable and internet won't be turned on until this afternoon. It actually explains why I wasn't making any progress with searching on my phone last night."

Meg massaged her temples, feeling a slight headache coming on. It was probably a toss-up between oversleeping and needing to eat.

"How am I supposed to figure out my living situation without the internet? I can easily dial the number to the company that took my money, but that's only one piece of the puzzle. I still need to look up places to potentially live."

Parker raised his shoulders up, then let them down again. "At this point, I'm thinking you might want to sit tight and wait until the cable company sets everything up. Or, there's always the library. If you want to hitch-hike eight miles across the island, that's on you. But I'd strongly suggest against it. Everything about you screams that you're from out of town."

Meg rolled her eyes. "Thanks, but I'm sure I can call the same taxi service that I used to get out here. It can't be that big of a deal."

Again, Parker smiled, and even shook his head as if he found her to be somewhat amusing. There was something electric that occurred whenever he looked her way. He had to have felt it too, because each time their eyes met, they both awkwardly looked away. *It also could've been the whole pajama situation*, she thought to herself.

"What's so funny?" she asked.

"Respectfully, I don't think I've ever come across anyone like you before. You're quite the pistol," he chuckled.

"What is that supposed to mean?"

"Well, I can tell you're from somebody's big city, the way you came in here, putting your foot down and demanding answers. You're lucky I didn't immediately kick you to the curb," he said, jokingly, but somehow it didn't come across nearly as funny to her.

Meg could feel her eyelids stretching wide open, not knowing what to say. So, she folded her arms instead.

He continued, "Perhaps we can continue this conversation later on. If I don't get going, I'm going to be late."

She watched as he jotted something on a flyer from the grocery store. "Here's my cell number if anything comes up. The appliances appear to be working just fine, so you can heat up your breakfast in the microwave. I should be back around noon."

He turned about face and proceeded to leave, yelling one last thing over his shoulder. "Oh, and if you need another night or two to get your plans in order, the invitation is open." Then he disappeared down the hall.

She didn't know whether to be insulted or excited about the extended time. So, for now, she shut the bedroom door behind her and dialed her father's number.

* * *

Luckily, Meg's dad was preoccupied in a meeting, leaving little time for a ton of questions. He always pushed himself with work, even though he was well beyond the threshold of retirement. There was something to be said about the love of a father. No matter how old she was, she'd always be his little girl. This situation was definitely one he probably wouldn't approve of. Therefore, she was happy to catch a break.

Following their call, she dialed the rental company. Hoping someone...anyone... would answer the phone. The phone lines were wide-open when she was interested in renting the place, so why would it be any different now?

But, once she dialed, "Of course not," was the only thing she could say aloud, feeling like even more of a fool than she had the night prior. This time there wasn't even a ring, just an annoying recording from the operator stating the line had been disconnected.

"Great!" she murmured, instantly recalling how it made her feel the time John called her naive. She remembered it like it was yesterday, handing a few bucks over to a homeless woman in the park. Something she'd always done when she came across someone in need. Only this time, they spotted the woman within the hour using the cash for a recreational beverage, something she didn't see coming. How could she? Besides, wasn't it supposed to be about the content of your heart, and putting others first that mattered most?

John thought it was the perfect lesson, teaching her to wise up and not be so quick to believe everyone she encountered. It was the classic case of not what he said, but how he said it that made her feel bad. Perhaps the real truth was she needed to wise up and get out of the relationship a lot earlier than she did. In hindsight, she'd much rather be with someone who was uplifting, instead of putting her down.

With limited options she began making a mental to-do list.

"Shower, eat, and make yourself useful around the house. Surely there's a mop and a dust pan around here. It's the least you can do considering he's allowing you to stay."

She flicked the light switch in the bathroom and pulled back the shower curtain. It was the only thing she hadn't explored after being so exhausted from her trip and a sleepless night.

With a twist of the faucet, she knew a shower was just what she needed. That combined with the sound of the ocean coming in through the shutters was the perfect recipe to help relax her mind.

Unfortunately, the pipe produced minimal bursts of water, and more of a knocking and combustion sound than anything else.

Meg closed her eyes and whispered, "Please help me out of this mess," then twisted the faucet back to the off position.

* * *

"Hey, Casey, do you have a spare minute?" Meg asked, silently releasing a few tears on her end of the line.

"Sure, I have a whole hour for you. I've been wondering how everything was going at your new beach house. Is it everything you hoped it would be?"

Meg wiped her tear-stained cheeks. "Can I get you to swear to secrecy?"

"Uh, oh. I hate it when you do that."

"I'm serious, Case. If you can't keep a tight lid on this one, then I won't share."

"You have my word," she sang. "What's wrong?"

Meg's lips trembled. "I think the real question is what's right? For starters, all the money I spent to rent the beach house is gone. Absolutely gone with nothing to show for it."

"What? No way."

"Yes, trust me, I'd give anything for this to be a joke. I was scammed out of thousands. Thousands! And, instead of me enjoying the crystal-clear blue water for a few days until work begins, I have to scramble to figure out where to go."

"Stop! So, where are you now?" Casey asked.

"At the beach house. It turns out the real owner is this investor guy who bought the place at an auction."

"Will he allow you to rent the house?"

Meg placed her on speaker so she could talk while she freely wandered about, giving herself another tour of the house in the daylight. "That would imply that I actually have money to spare. I'm down to my emergency savings, which is certainly not enough to cover the cost of renting this so-called luxury retreat."

"Meg, I can easily wire some cash to hold you over until you get paid."

"Thanks, I really appreciate it. And, trust me, if I get desperate, I may do just that. But, for now, I got myself into this mess, and I plan on getting myself out of it. I can hear John's voice just as plain as day, reminding me how—"

Casey interrupted, "stop right there. Don't do that to yourself. John's voice is no longer relevant, remember?"

"You're right."

As she strolled through the living room, she noticed a large painting of a secluded island hanging on the wall. It caught her attention, giving her that same tranquil feeling she had when she saw the ad for the rental.

Meg continued explaining, "it gets worse, Case."

"I don't know how much more I can take."

"The investor guy, his name is Parker," she said.

"Yeah."

"He's renovating the beach house and living here while he

works on the flip." Her voice dwindled down practically to a whisper. "He let me stay here last night. Well, in essence, I refused to leave until I verified that my rental agreement was truly non-existent."

"What? Are you crazy? You're staying in that house with a strange man you don't even know?" she asked in a very suggestive tone.

A few steps further, she entered the space where they ate last night, not quite a formal dining room, but still decorated with an empty pizza box and an empty soda can.

Meg rested her hand on the back of a wicker chair and glanced out at the endless view of the blue ocean in the back of the house. "Yep. Don't worry, I checked his deed and his license, and then locked myself in the bedroom last night just in case. It's not like I was able to get much sleep anyway. Not with a pending eviction at the forefront of my mind. Plus, I had a chance to talk to him last night. He really seems rather laid back, except for his occasional smart remarks." She smiled.

"Umm, I have to tell you, Meg. I'm glad you're not picking up serial killer vibes, but I'd still be way more comfortable if you weren't in this situation to begin with. I understand that you want clarification, and you lost a lot of money, but you're miles away from home."

Meg clenched at the sound of a vehicle making its way up the driveway. Knowing she wasn't expecting anyone, not at least until noon, she peered out the front shutters. Thankfully, her mind was put at ease when she saw it was only a mail truck.

Casey spoke on the other end of the line. "Meg, are you still there?"

"I'm here, and I heard everything you said. And, yes. I know I'm miles away from home. But that was the whole point, Case. To turn over a new leaf and fulfill a lifelong dream, remember? Is this a major setback? There's no doubt about it.

But I have to make this work. Besides, in just a few short days, I'll start my new job. Surely my new co-workers can help steer me in the right direction if I don't already have something figured out by then."

The silence on the other end of the line was deafening and lasted way longer than Meg could stand. Something would pan out, wouldn't it? Even if it was the craziest thing she'd ever done, a vote of confidence or support from her dear friend would've been nice right about now.

"Meg, you have to promise me you will call every single night until you get this situation straightened out. Do you hear me?"

Meg cracked a smile as she walked toward the back door, leading to her favorite getaway location. "Yes, I hear you loud and clear. It may not be a call every night, but I'll definitely send a text." She shook her head. "You're really starting to sound like my father, you know."

"If that's what it takes. I'll bet you didn't utter a single word of this to him. Did you?" Casey pressed.

"No, but I did give him an overview of the place. Plus, he was in a meeting, so we couldn't really talk long."

Outside was a picture-perfect view of the way Meg imagined her mornings would be. She'd already witnessed a beautiful sunset, but the crashing waves, the crystal blue water, and the sound of the birds chirping was like heaven. Something she'd only dreamed of until now.

"Casey, would you listen to this?" Meg held her phone up, hoping to amplify the sound.

"I hear it. I'm sure it's everything you ever wanted and more. However, my mind won't feel at ease until we have the guy checked out. I want you to text me his name and any other pertinent information you can find. I'll have the hubby do a little digging around to make sure he's not on a wanted list somewhere."

Meg chuckled. "Oh, come on, Case. He seems genuine, and he's been very nice, although technically, he doesn't really have to be. He even showed me the deed, and everything matched up with his license. If he were really on some sort of crime spree, do you think he'd willingly share that kind of information?"

"I don't care. Call it second nature after being married to a cop for fifteen years, but if he's everything you say he is, then his record should come back squeaky clean."

"Okay. Whatever you say, Detective Casey. I have his license number and his date of birth. I'll send it to you as soon as we get off," Meg replied.

"See, look at that. You're just as leery as I am."

"Not really. Just being thorough, that's all."

Looking down at her pajamas, Meg was reminded that she still needed to get dressed, eat, and try to sketch out a game plan.

Although inviting, the waves, and the long stretch of beach would have to wait.

Chapter 5

Parker

Parker Wilson pushed the front door open with his elbow, carrying a heavy box containing a pot belly grill. He left several bags of groceries on the front porch and placed the box down. Immediately he noticed a sun-filled living room that had been cleaned, with the ceiling fan generating a gentle breeze. The place smelled more like lemon products than the old dingy odor that consumed the air just one evening prior.

He froze, listening for a sign of movement coming from his house guest. But, with no indicator that she was around, he continued unloading the car and bringing bags in.

"Hello? Anybody home?" he called out.

Feeling somewhat curious about where she could be, he wandered down the hall, noticing her door was left open. Her bed was made up, and the sheets tightly tucked in hotel style. For a moment, he wondered where she even found a clean set of sheets. He certainly could've used a set for himself while laying across a dusty mattress last night.

Then, there was the grocery flyer from this morning with

his number written on it, neatly placed on the nightstand adjacent to her bed. The place had the touch of a woman, something he hadn't experienced in a long time.

"Looking for something?" she asked, this time startling the daylights out of him.

"Yes. No. Well, yes, actually. When you didn't respond, I came back here to check and see if everything was okay."

Parker couldn't help but glance at her coral toe nails, decorated flip flops, and a floral dress that was fit for the island. He swallowed, forcing his eyes to meet hers, instead of staring at her smooth legs. "I picked up a few things after the meeting and was bringing everything in," he stuttered.

"I can tell. You left the front door wide open, so I brought in the rest of the bags for you. I don't want to tell you how to live your life, but if I were you, I'd be a bit more conscious about going around leaving everything unlocked. Your car, the front door. This may be the Bahamas, but crime exists everywhere, you know."

Parker chuckled. "Uh, thanks for the advice. However, this beach house happens to be tucked away in one of the safest areas on the island. No one, and I mean no one, comes through here that I don't already know. I've flipped houses in the area before."

He watched as she turned about-face, making her way back toward the living area.

Meg pointed toward him. "Yeah, well I'd still be aware. I pulled up in a taxi cab and you didn't hear a thing. On another note, I wish I could say the same about the safety of the area I visited today. The address for the property management company led me to a sketchy little ally, neatly tucked away off the beaten path of Bay Street. The building was toward the end of a drag where there's a lot of tourist shopping. But somehow the ally felt more like a dark den with storefronts as a cover up for conducting illegal activity. It looked awfully shady, if you know what I mean."

Parker ran the palm of his hand down his face in utter disbelief. "You went there by yourself?"

"Yes. How else was I supposed to figure out what's going on? I just couldn't sit around here all morning and do nothing. After you left, I cleaned up as best as I could, as a thank you for letting me stay, but I needed to get out there. As it turns out, it was nothing but a wasted effort, which is a horrible feeling, especially knowing that it's Friday and I start my new job on Monday morning."

Parker felt frustrated for her. Not a reaction he was expecting, but then again, life had been filled with the unexpected since the moment he arrived.

"Okay, look. Logic tells me to stay out of this. Clearly, you're a grown woman and if you made it this far, all the way from — wherever you're from, then you'll figure this thing out."

"But?" she asked.

He squinted at her for a second, before proceeding. "But the very fabric of who I am is begging you not to do that again. I'd feel terrible to learn that someone under my watch fell victim to a senseless crime. Even if you just got lost. It's not worth it. Next time you want to go somewhere to check things out, say something to me. I could've given you a ride."

Parker casually began unpacking some orange juice, a few steaks, and other groceries, noticing even the refrigerator was a far sight better than how it looked yesterday. He didn't know how she did it, but this beach house that hadn't been cared for was starting to look like a vacation home again. If she could manage to be that productive, squeezing in everything, including an adventurous taxi ride downtown, maybe it was worth it to keep her around. Perhaps she wouldn't make such a bad housemate after all.

What am I thinking? How can two people be housemates in a beach house that's about to be renovated?

Meg snarled at him. "Under your watch? Ha, that's funny! Just yesterday you were telling me that I needed to make other arrangements."

"Yes, but that was before we talked. This morning I extended the invitation for you to stay a few more days, and, although I can't believe I'm saying this —"

She waved, looking as if she were at her tipping point. "Please, don't do me any favors. It's not like this new adventure I've embarked upon could get any worse than it already has. Let's see. How has it gone so far? Oh, that's right, I remember. —" She started to pace. "First, my fiancé of three years broke things off by telling me he was cheating. That happened just days before our wedding. Yay, for me! Granted, a three-year engagement should've been a clue that something wasn't going right, but me being the hopeless romantic that I am, still went along with the program. Then, in an effort to give myself a fresh start, I chose to focus on my career and my dream job of working at a five-star island resort. The Cove! Have you heard of it?"

He paused, feeling a little nervous to speak, so instead he nodded.

"Yeah, well, that's where I'll be working. One would think I'd finally made it to the big leagues, accepting a director's position in the sales department, but do you think I can get excited about it, or even enjoy this weekend as I prepare to start on Monday? Noooooo, of course not. Why? Because I took almost every last dime of that three-carat diamond ring and spent it on a bogus beach house that doesn't exist. And now —"

She broke down, releasing an unexpected floodgate of tears. "That jerk," she muttered under her breath.

Parker didn't know if he should offer words of comfort, or if she wanted to be consoled or what. So, he did what came naturally, pulling out a chair and grabbing a roll of paper towels to offer.

She laughed. "Thank you. Although, I don't think the whole roll will be necessary."

He was grateful something as small as a paper towel could make her smile again.

"Hey, at least you can't say I never offered you anything," he chuckled.

"This is true. You've been more than gracious. And, if I'm being realistic, it's obvious I have nothing to gain here. This place is completely yours, as you've already proven. My mishap has nothing to do with you; therefore, I'll be moving out before the end of the weekend."

Parker contemplated, already knowing he'd rather figure something out with her, but he didn't want to come off too strong.

"What about the delivery of your belongings? Where will you stay?"

"Good question," Meg replied, while patting her eyes.

"Listen. It sounds like you've had a rough few weeks, leading up to now." He looked around, assessing just how much work had to be done.

"I'm sure the best-case scenario would've been to have this house all to yourself, but if you're willing to make the best of it, you're more than welcome to camp out here for a while. At least until you have time to start your job and get a solid game plan lined up for your new living situation."

She slowly raised her head, making eye contact. "You sure you don't mind?"

Parker nodded. "As long as you don't mind what's to come. Drop cloths lying around, no access to the pool area. It's going to be a real work zone. Do you think you're up for it?"

He watched as she seemed uncertain about what to do. But after a few moments, Meg's infectious grin emerged, making him smile along with her.

"It's a deal. Can I pay you a weekly rate for the room once I start receiving a paycheck, if that's okay?" she asked.

"I'm sure we can work something out. Oh, and before I forget, it's likely you'll see my sister around here pretty soon, so get ready. She usually helps me with choosing color patterns and tiles. And, since an arrangement like this, on a worksite, is out of character for me, I'm sure she'll poke around and ask a few questions."

"Protective family?" she smiled.

"Yes and no. For the most part our parents were always open to taking people in and helping out when needed. They used to host plenty of the guys from college, foreign exchange students, and random people in need over the years. Just knowing my sister and her curious nature, this will strike her as different."

Meg rose from her chair and gazed out the back door to the area where he originally found her. That moment still secretly made him smile on the inside. Did she really think he'd feel threatened by her holding a sundial in her hand?

She whipped around. "What area of the house will you begin working on first?"

"You were just looking at it. The pool is dated and needs a fresh new look. It's one of the more expensive projects on the list with all the surrounding stone, but a wonderful selling point once the job is complete. My contractor is stopping by on Monday to take a look."

Parker joined her, standing side by side, looking toward the pool. "Come outside with me for a minute and tell me what you think."

From the deck he pointed toward the old stone that needed

replacing and the interior tile that would be removed. The whole time noticing her hair as it blew in the wind, a different pair of earrings that decorated her neck, just so, and a distinct beauty mark behind her left ear.

To describe her looks as breath-taking was an understatement. An added layer was a warmth that existed between them. A familiar warmth like he used to experience with Jenna.

Jenna Maxwell was the woman he planned to spend the rest of his life with. Sadly, she'd passed away.

"I'd love to have an outsider's opinion. If you were buying this house for yourself, would you be happy with my plans for the pool or...?" he asked.

"Honestly?"

He smiled. "Of course, I want honesty. If this is supposed to be a money-maker, then I need all the honesty I can get. Women know how to add their loving touch when it comes to designing a home. Tell me what you think."

"Okay, then. If it were me, I'd add a jacuzzi. It's in the budget. That way buyers have a choice of amenities with the beach as their backdrop." Meg spoke, envisioning her idea as she pointed toward the pool. "Again, if it's too much for the budget, then another cost-effective approach would be to include some other cool effects, like in-ground nightlights, or surround-sound for entertainment. Something that shows you put a lot of thought and care into the design. Trust me, families will love it."

Was it wrong of him to watch her lips as she described her vision? Was it wrong that he was curious about her personal life and everything she'd been through, leading her to this moment? These were the questions reeling around in his mind, but he tried his best not to let it show.

Meg interrupted. "Hello? Earth to Mars. Any thoughts about my suggestions?"

"Yeah, I think your ideas are great. I was just wondering why I didn't think of them myself. The house was built in the late nineties, so of course, surround-sound wasn't exactly at the top of the list for entertainment. At least not in this model, it wasn't. Even the jacuzzi idea. If I could manage to shift a few coins around, I bet I could make it work. I can at least have Miguel price it out for me. Thank you for the ideas."

Meg smiled really big as if she was pleased to be of service. "No problem. My advice normally comes with a fee, but since you were nice enough to let me stay here, it's free of charge."

He laughed, pleasantly enjoying her sense of humor. "Have you been down to the beach yet?" he asked.

"Oddly enough, no. It was at the top of my list of things to do when I arrived. I think you walked in and caught me taking in the view. After that, everything seemed to go downhill."

"Well, I have a suggestion." He looked at his watch. "We have about an hour before someone from the cable company arrives, and I definitely need to take a walk down and get a good look at the house from the back. Would you like to join me?" he asked.

Meg looked as if she were considering the idea, but hesitated. "Um, I was thinking about unpacking the rest of my things. I can always —"

"Wait a minute. You're not uncomfortable around me, are you? Not after adventuring halfway across the island to the sketchiest part of town. Remember, I'm the guy who proved that I actually belong here," he teased but meant every word of it.

"I know. It's the New Yorker in me. I'm a city girl as you mentioned. Some of us are born suspicious. Plus, I'm still getting used to the whole housemate idea. Can't say I've ever done anything like this before."

Parker extended his hand to shake hers. "I promise, you can

feel at ease around me. My record is squeaky clean, and my mother raised me to be a gentleman. Those two things alone mean a lot to me. I wouldn't dare do anything to damage my reputation or disrespect you.

Meg took a deep breath. "Okay, then. The beach awaits. Please, lead the way."

One thing he knew for certain; he was already intrigued by the adventurous city-girl. For someone who was supposed to be focused on renovations, all he could seem to think about was her.

Chapter 6

Meg

"I absolutely refuse to fall for this guy. Refuse, refuse, refuse! Do you hear me?" Meg paced around her bedroom, whispering into the phone, and pointing daggers in the air as she spoke to her best friend Casey.

"Okayyyy. One would hope you're not contemplating falling in love. Especially since you just arrived and barely know anything about him."

Meg took a deep breath. "Exactly! But, usually that's how it all begins. Girl meets new guy... new guy is cute. No — in this case, it's more like new guy is hot! First, you get to talking and sharing your life stories together and then, voila! Just like that, something hits you over the head, leaving you in a state of pure stupidity. No! I'm not falling for it this time, Casey. I refuse."

"Meg."

"What?"

"Would you like to start by hearing about his background check, first?"

Immediately, Meg backed down, easing her breathing into

more of a normal rhythm. "Yes, of course. How did you manage to come up with a report on a Sunday afternoon?"

Casey snickered on the other end of the line. "Honey, the police station is open twenty-four-seven. Craig started his shift a couple of hours ago, so he was able to do some poking around."

"Right. So, did he find anything?"

"No. Not even a traffic violation. The guy is telling you the truth about who he is, that's for certain. It looks like he had a life in Chicago prior to moving to the Bahamas. At least, his name popped up with a Chicago address from over four years ago. Did he mention anything about it?"

"Yes, he did. He told me a little about his family and his sister who lives out here. I'm just glad that everything checks out. The last thing I need to worry about is living with an ex-convict, or a psychopath," she teased.

Casey agreed. "Uh, that's exactly why I had Craig look him up. The only other thing that stood out was he once lived at an address in Nassau with a lady by the name of Jenna Maxwell. Did her name ever come up?"

Meg thought for a moment. "No, but I also haven't been here long enough to dig into his whole life story."

"If that's the case, then what has you all stirred up? Is he that good looking?"

Meg didn't want to tell Casey about her dream or about their awkward eye communication this morning, so instead she rolled her eyes and flopped backwards onto the bed. "Good looking is an understatement. But that's only half the story. Case, you know I'm still raw from everything that happened with John. The last thing I need is a kind, respectful, gentle, and handsome single man coming to my aid."

Casey continued pressing her. "How do you know that he's single?"

"Well, I presume he's single given the only women he's mentioned are his sisters and his mother."

Meg could still hear the kids playing in the background, but she noticed Casey hadn't said a word.

"Hello?"

"I'm here, Meg. To be honest, you have to do as you're led. If it were me, I'd be focused on enjoying my life starting right now. So what, you met a cute guy and you're starting to enjoy his company. There's nothing wrong with that. It's the first guy you've met. Your stay will be temporary, and then you'll be on your way, potentially meeting the next guy soon after. Your stay is temporary, isn't it?"

"Ugh, that's a story in itself. We made an agreement that would allow me to stay for a little while longer, at least until I get my bearings, and start getting paid. So now, my dream beach rental has turned into a makeshift room rental with pending renovations, but it will do."

"Oh, boy. Well, all I can tell you is try and find a way to make the best of it. As I offered earlier, you always have a guest room waiting for you here in New York. If you would fess up and be forthright with your dad, I'm sure he'd offer a place for you as well."

Meg held her head. "Don't worry. The next time we speak I'll share everything with him. I needed reassurance from Craig's police report first."

Casey laughed. "I'm sure you did."

"Hey, Case, thanks for always being an ear whenever I need to vent. I don't know how I always manage to wind up in these interesting situations. But I promise, this time will be very different. I'm done with dating, period. You'd think somehow by thirty-nine it would get a little easier, but no. For some of us it only gets worse."

"Meg, I wish you'd stop being so hard on yourself. For as

long as I've known you, you've always been your own worst critic, expecting nothing short of perfection at all times." Meg silently agreed on her end of the line, allowing Casey to continue.

"Unfortunately, everything can't be perfect. It's time you start cutting yourself some slack."

"I know, Case. I'm just tired of the same old, same old. I really thought John was the one. In hindsight, I don't know why I believed such a lie, but I did."

"Maybe it's because you're human?"

Meg chuckled. "Yeah, well, this human feels depleted and stripped of the ability to love again. That's why I'm making it official. I'm going to be laser focused on becoming the top sales director this resort has ever had and making a great life for myself here in the Bahamas. Who knows? I might even consider buying my own house on the beach someday. Either way, I'm going to focus on being the best Meg Carter I can be. Something that can certainly be done without including a man in my life!"

Chapter 7

Meg

On Monday, Meg stepped out of the taxi onto the cobblestone entrance of the resort. "Welcome to The Cove," a man greeted her, looking for luggage to carry.

"Are you staying with us as a guest at the resort?" he asked. She noticed he wore slacks and a polo with the resort's name embroidered on the front.

"Me? Oh no. I'm a new employee. Meg Carter, Director of Sales, nice to meet you," she extended her hand.

"Ah, Miss Meg. Yes, it's nice to meet you as well. My name is Louis. I was told that you would be arriving this morning, and you're early. This is wonderful. Please, allow me to escort you to Miss Delilah, our Director of Human Resources. She's excited to meet you in person." he explained, shaking her hand enthusiastically the entire time he spoke.

"Perfect, Louis. Thank you."

Meg took a moment to look around, taking in the palm trees, a relaxing trade wind, and the warmth of the Bahama

Breeze, all serving as signs that she'd made it. Day one of her life-long dream was about to begin.

Once the sliding glass doors detected their presence, she felt a rush of cool air conditioning and observed a huge fountain at the center of the grand atrium.

"Do you mind if I stop to snap a quick picture in front of the fountain? I just want to document my first day." She smiled.

"Sure, go right ahead, miss."

After the picture, Louis escorted her down a hall that led to a set of office doors. She was grateful for packing a pencil leg skirt with enough elasticity to make her feel comfortable, and her favorite pumps that were very easy-going on the feet.

A woman dressed almost like a stewardess in navy pumps greeted them outside the door labeled HR. "Good morning, darlin. You must be Meg Carter."

Meg smiled. "Yes, nice to meet you, Mrs. —"

"Oh, please, call me Frankie. We're very relaxed and informal among the staff." Then she turned to Louis. "Thank you so much for delivering Meg to us. Delilah was pulled onto a conference call. She promised to join us within the hour."

Louis nodded. "Again, Miss Carter. Welcome. I'm sure I'll see you around soon." He waved, and Meg returned the welcoming gesture.

Frankie raised her hand to her hip. "Stylish from head to toe, just like I expected from a New Yorker." She pointed to Meg's shoes. "Let me guess, those shoes you're wearing are designed by —"

Meg laughed. "Ha, I can stop you right there. I aim to look the part without breaking the bank account. No fancy brands here. I'm just a regular girl living on a budget."

"My kind of girl, indeed. When I heard we were getting somebody from New York I was so excited. I used to live there for a year with my cousin. It's the most expensive city I've ever visited, but boy did I have a good time!"

Frankie checked over her shoulder. "Now, because Delilah had to hop on a conference call, she asked me to give you a tour of the resort. We have about an hour to peruse the grounds. So, you have two choices. Do you want the behind the scenes, fun tour, where I show you the resort's best kept secrets? Or, do you want the traditional tour, similar to the one we give our guests?"

Meg's eyes widened. "Uhh, how about a little of both?"

"Ah, so you're adventurous. I like it. Follow me. We'll start outdoors and make our way around from there."

Outside, Meg strolled beside Frankie as she followed a path leading toward the first pool. "We have over ten pools located around the resort. Every one of them offer nearby access to beach towels, umbrellas, and eateries. In just a little while, every chair will be filled with sun worshippers, lathering themselves in sunscreen and basking in the sun."

Meg stopped, taking in the sound of a waterfall and the gorgeous view of tall palm trees surrounding the area. "I remember seeing this online when I was conducting research about the job. Gosh, there's nothing like being here and seeing it in person."

Frankie smiled. "I'll bet. If you think this is something, wait until you see the beachside of the resort. It's so relaxing when I come out here for lunch. Sometimes, I have to set an alarm so I don't fall asleep."

"I'll bet," Meg replied.

They continued over a bridge leading down to the nearest beach. It was one of five access points all connecting to the resort.

"When did you arrive to the Bahamas?" Frankie asked.

"Last Thursday evening, and it's been quite the adventure

ever since. My boxes haven't even arrived yet. They won't be delivered for another two days."

Frankie nodded, then pointed down toward a long stretch. "Do you see that area over there?"

"Mm hmm."

Frankie held her finger to her lips. "Don't tell Delilah I told you so, but that area of the beach is like a hidden gem for the staff of the resort. If you ever need to get away, the guests never seem to wander down this far. It's like our own little slice of heaven that we get to enjoy without work related interruptions. Somehow, if you notice staff members magically disappearing for an hour or so, this is usually where you can find them," she chuckled.

"Good to know. Although, I would imagine I'll be so immersed in all things related to sales, I doubt I'll have time," Meg replied.

"Yeah, but if you're ever having a stressful day, at least you know you have options. Now, back to what you were saying. So, your boxes don't arrive for a couple of days, but clearly you packed well for the trip. You look fabulous."

Meg tugged on her blazer, making sure it fit just so. "Why, thank you."

The sun felt so good, she really wanted to peel out of her business attire and head down to the shore.

"Did you find a nice place to live?" Frankie asked.

Meg thought better of getting into the details of her living arrangement and mishap with the rental. She didn't want her new co-workers second guessing her judgment.

"Oh, I found a little beach house over at Seaside Point. It's a temporary spot, but it will do for now."

Frankie paused. "Swanky! Seaside Point is definitely not for the budget conscious. You must be doing very well to be living over there!"

Meg could tell she and Frankie would become fast friends, or at the least, fast work buddies. They were hitting it off well, and she yearned to have that kind of connection with somebody on the island as she began to settle in.

"Trust me, I'll have to save the story of how I ended up at Seaside Point for another time, but while I'm there, I definitely plan to enjoy it as much as I can."

They continued walking, this time Meg taking over in the question asking department. "Do you have family and friends out here?"

"My family lives in England, but I have three wonderful girlfriends that are so close, I consider them like family. One evening, if you're not busy, you should come out with us. We're not big party girls or anything, but we'll take you to the best eateries on the island and get lost in girl-talk until the sun rises if you let us," she smiled.

"Sounds like my kind of girls."

Frankie pulled out a set of keys and hopped into a miniature golf cart. "Hop in. We might want to take the rest of this tour in the cart. If not, you'll end up sweating in your nice suit as the sun has a tendency to heat up really quick around here."

Meg buckled herself in and held on as she pulled out of the parking space. "So, can I ask you a question?"

"Sure, you can ask as many questions as you'd like," Frankie responded.

"What brought you to the Bahamas if your family lives in the UK?"

Frankie smiled. "I'm embarrassed to admit it was virtual love."

The two looked at each other, then burst out into a serious bout of laughter.

"I'm so sorry. I didn't mean to laugh, but I have never heard anyone say that before. I guess there's a first time for everything," Meg confessed.

"Yes, this is true. However, in this case it's exactly as it sounds. I met him online and everything about him was very promising. His career, his age, we had a lot in common, and we consistently spoke online for months. I'm talking almost a solid year before I finally caved and committed to coming here and seeing him. To this day, I'm certain that was the first wrong move I made."

Meg was intrigued. She loved how candid Frankie was being about her experience.

Frankie steered down a path passing by an outdoor yoga class. "I should've stayed put and allowed him to make the effort to come and see me. Rule number one when it comes to long distance online dating, make the man do the traveling. At least initially."

"Well, now you have me really curious," Meg replied.

"It's the classic case of moving here sight unseen. Turns out the guy was a fraud. He didn't have a job and didn't even live where he claimed to live. I guess he never expected me to come out here. Heck, I never expected I would do such a thing, but here I am."

"I'm sorry."

She shook her head in disagreement. "There's nothing to be sorry about. You live and you learn. I was foolish to believe him, but the story doesn't end there. I decided to stay and make a great life for myself right here on the island. I promised myself I would give it six solid months, and now look. I'm still here, two years later. I survived. And, I still believe that someday I could meet Mr. Right."

Meg held her hand out. "Can you rub some of that on me?"

"What?"

"That positive outlook of yours. I need a healthy dose of

whatever it is you're taking," she laughed.

Frankie pointed upward to the open sky. "My grandmother used to tell me if you believe in Him, you'll be just fine, darlin. You'll be just fine!"

"Your grandmother sounds like a very wise woman."

Frankie swerved the cart around the perimeter of the resort, pausing alongside a sprawling golf course. "She was a very wise woman. But, she has her angel wings now. I'd give anything to be able to see her again. I would imagine if she were here, she would've had a lot to say about my venture to the island. She probably would've tried to stop me. You see, the only reason why I met that guy was because I gave in to my impatience and signed up for one of those ridiculous dating apps. I was so ready to meet 'the one' and gave into a fantasy instead of allowing things to happen naturally," she chuckled. "I should be embarrassed. Listen to me carrying on about my personal life and we just met."

Meg offered a few words of reassurance. "I don't mind. It's easy to talk when you meet someone that you share things in common with. Plus, I can already tell, you and I are like sisters from a different mother," she laughed.

"True. True indeed!" Frankie pointed toward the golf course. "Well, my dear sister friend, when Delilah asks about our tour, I want us to have a valid response. So, let's continue, shall we?"

"Absolutely. Let me guess, this is the golf course, a place where I hope to bring in a lot of tournaments, along with bringing in business to the banquet halls, the spas, you name it."

Meg envisioned applying her past experience to help bring new business to the resort, sending their revenue bursting through the roof. With the right connections, skills, and know-how, she'd even bring some of her old clients to the islands to host events. If things went according to plan, The Cove would see results like they'd never seen before.

Frankie's big smile was contagious. "You don't need me to give you a tour. What you need is the keys to your office so you can get started. Watch out Cove Resort, Meg Carter is taking us to the next level." They giggled. "And, hopefully, helping us to earn bonus checks while she's at it."

* * *

The remainder of the day was filled with processing, fingerprinting and paperwork, meet and greets, and at the conclusion, a fifteen-minute taxi ride back to the beach house. Meg would have to do something about the daily expense of catching a taxi back and forth. One thought was purchasing a used car, but getting used to driving on the opposite side of the vehicle might be a bit of a challenge.

Meg tipped the driver and began the hike up the long driveway but froze in place at the sight in front of her. "You're kidding me," she whispered.

It wasn't the overgrown weeds that caught her attention, or Parker's pick-up truck filled with lumber, or the additional red truck parked beside his. Instead, it was boxes upon boxes stacked on the front porch, clearly delivered by the moving company, without her knowing.

"Perfect timing," Parker said, as he lifted one of the boxes. Another gentleman followed, exiting the house with a notepad in hand and a pencil wedged behind his ear. He acknowledged her and then spoke to Parker.

"As I said earlier, I can get my guys out here and start the job by the end of the week, but the price is pretty firm. With the cost of materials going up, that's about the best I can do."

They bantered back and forth a bit, Parker looking noticeably handsome in his shorts and t-shirt that revealed his muscles.

"Alright, man. Let me make a few phone calls and sit down and crunch the numbers again. I'll get back to you in the morning." Parker nodded toward Meg. "Forgive my manners, Miguel. This is Meg."

Parker left the introduction open-ended, with no explanation as to who she was. It was the sort of thing men did when they proudly introduced their other half. Except, she didn't hold that title. When no further explanation followed, she just waved. "Hi, Miguel. Pleased to meet you. I'm going to get out of your way. It looks as if I have quite a few boxes to tend to."

Parker dismissed the idea. "Why don't you head inside and kick your shoes off? I'll finish taking care of the boxes as soon as I'm done talking to Miguel."

With each step that she took closer to the front porch, Meg didn't know what to think about Parker Wilson. She kept telling herself he was a stranger. She hadn't been used to someone being kind for no reason, not unless they were a close relative or friend. *What was his motive?* Maybe it was her suspicious nature making it difficult for her to accept his generosity. Who knows? And, how about the casual way he introduced her and sent her inside to go relax? She wasn't his woman. Perhaps it was time they had a chat to help lay some ground rules.

Inside, she changed into a comfortable outfit suitable for moving boxes and threw on her tennis shoes. After tying her hair up, she returned to find Parker bringing more boxes inside, two at a time.

"Thanks for your help, but you can leave the rest of the boxes. I'll take over from here."

"Oh, it's nothing. As I said earlier, kick up your feet and relax. You just got in from your first day. I can stack these around the living room and leave them there until you're ready to sort through everything." He continued, busily walking back and forth, barely breaking a sweat. Even in the eighty-six-degree weather he wasn't missing a beat. The man was obviously fit as he had a six-pack that showed through his shirt.

"It's okay, really. I have it. I'm not a damsel in distress kind of woman. My parents raised me to fend for myself when necessary."

Parker laid the box he was holding down and gave her a look. "Uh, well, my parents raised me to be a gentleman. If I ever let my mother or sisters walk through a door without holding it, or lift anything heavy without help, my father would've knocked me into next week. Therefore, no harm intended," he explained. "Why the sudden shift? Did I do something wrong? I can easily just stay out of your way, although that might be weird given that we live here together."

Immediately she felt like a jerk. "You didn't do anything." She sighed. "If anything, you're being very helpful. Look, I might as well just go ahead and say everything I'm thinking out loud, that way there's no awkwardness between us."

Parker interrupted. "I know, you've been through a lot. It's okay."

"No, you should hear me out. I'm not used to a man bending over backwards to be kind to me. It's not your fault, but the last man I was with was way too preoccupied with himself."

His eyebrows folded together. "Okay."

Meg pointed toward the boxes. "Then, there's this unexpected surprise. It seems like ever since I landed the only thing that's gone right is my first day of work, thankfully. But these boxes weren't supposed to be delivered until a couple of days from now, and I specifically arranged it so I could be home to receive them. Surely the moving companies out here know a thing or two about customer service!"

He revealed a partial smile. "Most people I know would be happy to have their things early. It's not exactly the worst thing they could've ever happened," he teased.

"True." She gave in to his sense of humor, laughing at herself, while appreciating his ability to help her relax.

"Is there anything else on your mind? I'd hate to do anything else that would be received as offensive. I'm sure the moving company would say the same."

Meg folded her arms and pointed one foot outward to show that she was on to his jokes. "No! There's nothing else on my mind. Actually, perhaps just one thing."

"Let me have it," he said.

"Are you sure my being here for a little while won't be a burden? I mean, you have Miguel here, and I'm sure lots of others will be on site. Plus, I've yet to see one house flipping show that involved a tenant renting out a room."

Parker moved closer to where she was standing. Not too close to invade her space, but enough for her to breathe a trace of his cologne and make her stomach flutter.

"Can we make a deal?" he asked.

"Sure."

"Good. How about we discuss this over grilled steaks, this evening, right after I'm done pulling the weeds out front? In my family, everything gets resolved over a home cooked meal. Agreed?"

Meg tilted her head, certainly not expecting an invite for steaks. "Uh, sure. Okay. Do you need any help with the yard?"

"Nope. The only thing I need is you and your appetite, on the beach, around seven-ish."

Is he asking me out on a date? No, Meg, stop while you're ahead. It's just two adults eating dinner in the backyard, on a romantic beach. No biggy.

Chapter 8

Parker

Parker Wilson jabbed his fork into the last piece of steak, thoroughly excited to see Meg consuming what he prepared. With the sunset as their backdrop and the Bahama breeze, it was the perfect evening to be outside.

"I have an idea, but it requires a little trust on your part," he offered.

"Uh oh, should I be nervous?" Meg chuckled.

"Not at all. I was just thinking, if you're feeling a little adventurous, we could hop in the truck and take a ten-minute drive. I'd like to show you something that will hopefully give you a little inspiration. Maybe along the way you can tell me about your first day at work."

She relaxed in her chair and comfortably crossed her legs, igniting in him an undeniable urge to know more about her.

"I do have to rise and shine early in the morning, you know. I don't officially start alternating working from home days until I've been there at least a month."

He nodded. "Oh, come on. Humor me, a little. What's the

sense in taking on the adventure of moving out here if you don't do anything spontaneous and fun?"

Meg looked around. "Okay, fine. I can spare an hour, but then I must get ready for work."

"Okay," he replied, leaping to his feet.

She wore a smirk on her face as she prepared to speak again. "And one more thing."

"What's that?"

"If I comply and go along with this adventure of yours, you must agree to share the rest of your story. You know, the one you started to tell over pizza about why you're single and moving around like a nomad instead of settling down with a family."

"Ha! You really drive a hard bargain."

She had him there. However, if that was the key to unlocking all the layers that she was hiding behind, he was willing to give it a shot.

* * *

The bumpy twist and turns in his pickup took them along the hillside of the island. Parker occasionally slowed down, passing colorful homes, and pointing out every one he'd renovated. "You see that one over there, nestled in the hills?"

"Yeah."

"I renovated that house, along with the blue one coming up just before we get to our destination," he explained.

"Nice. You've been pretty busy. How many houses have you renovated?"

"Eight over the course of three years. Technically nine, but I didn't do the first one by myself. My goal is to ramp things up in the new year. If things go according to plan, I'm going to settle into one of my renovations and call it home."

She looked surprised. "Really? The nomad life is starting to get kind of lame, is it?"

"Hey, do I hear an air of sarcasm in your tone?" He teased. "You can make fun of me all you want but living like a nomad helped pay the bills. If you think about it, I've remained within the same five- or six-mile radius, getting to know the culture and the locals very well. And I don't know anyone who would complain about living the beach life on a gorgeous island while making a living. It doesn't get any better than this."

He noticed her distinct dimples and hazel eyes as Meg looked toward him and smiled. "I'll give you this much. The atmosphere here beats living in New York City any day of the week."

Parker's eyebrows raised. "Ah, somebody just admitted to being from New York City... I knew it! I knew you were a city girl from the moment we met."

Meg twirled her finger in the air. "Yeah, yeah, yeah... you're just saying that because I was giving you a hard time in the beginning."

"As you should give any guy a hard time at first. A real man should earn your trust and respect, I get it."

He noticed her pausing at his last statement but didn't comment.

Parker guided the wheel to the right with the palm of his right hand, pulling completely off the road to the most breath-taking sight, causing Meg to gasp.

"This is beautiful. My goodness, I don't think I've ever seen anything like it."

He shifted the gear in park and turned off the engine. "This little spot is overlooking the purest white sand stretching for miles and miles, and crystal-clear water just like they advertise in the brochures. And, wait for it – do you hear that sound?" he asked with his arms opened wide.

"The sound of the ocean?"

Parker closed his eyes. "Yes. It's so serene. So therapeutic."

"We can have that wonderful sound every day at the house. I mean, for the time-being, while I'm there. But this cliff overlooking the beach is like a small taste of heaven. And, inspiring, just like you said it would be," she replied.

"Would you like to get out for a few minutes? Maybe take a look around."

"Sure," she replied.

Parker pushed his sunglasses back and hoisted himself on a rock. Being the free spirit in nature came naturally whenever he didn't have to wear a suit and tie. He couldn't make sense of it, but being around Meg made him want to be even more free. He wanted to open up and talk. A feeling he hadn't experienced since Jenna died.

"I suppose since you held up your end of the deal, it's time that I hold up mine," he said.

As Meg found another rock to make herself comfortable, he began talking. "It's pretty simple really. I moved out here to be closer to my sister and her family –"

"That's right, the sister who helps you design the houses, correct?"

"Correct. Not long after I moved here to be closer to family, I met the woman of my dreams, fell in love, and was engaged to be married."

He could see a dreaded look starting to form on Meg's face. It never failed. With the few he did share his story with, their facial expressions always started out hopeful, then eventually eased into a more somber look as they realized what he was about to say.

"What happened?" she asked.

"She was diagnosed with lymphoma, and it was pretty

advanced. It took her out of here so fast it made me question whether there really is a God."

Meg stopped. "Parker, I'm so sorry."

"It's okay. At the time that was just my way of coping. I was angry. Very angry. Especially because I knew I was a good person and didn't deserve that kind of loss. Looking back, that was kind of selfish of me, really. It wasn't about me. Jenna was the one who didn't deserve that kind of sickness, but sadly these kinds of things are unavoidable. Now, after time and healing, I see things much differently. I know without a doubt if God didn't exist, my ability to heal would be non-existent."

He caught a glimpse of Meg wiping her eyes. "It's okay. Really. I've come a long way from where I used to be," he said.

She turned toward the gentle breeze. "Just hearing your story makes me feel like my past relationship issues were very trivial in comparison."

Parker sat upright. "You shouldn't compare. Your pain and suffering are just as valid as anyone else's." He stood up and faced the picturesque view of the sun that was beginning to set. A view he could watch over and over again, and it still never got old.

"Parker, when does it ever stop?"

"The pain?" he asked.

For the first time Meg let down her guard, relinquishing everything that she'd been holding back. "Yes, the pain. When does it ever go away? Sometimes, I think if I just learn how to suppress it long enough it will just disappear or I'll grow numb to it. Neither option is good, but it's all I have to work with at this point."

Reflecting back, he could recall being in the same position. Not knowing what to do with his emotions, some days feeling like he was moments away from throwing in the towel.

"While I'm no expert, I know one thing that helped was

taking things one day at a time. Getting on my knees about it. Waking up each day, and facing whatever was before me. Try not to worry about the rest, although I know it sounds easier said than done, you have to start somewhere."

Meg joined him, facing the sunset, looking as if she was carrying the weight of the world on her shoulders. "I think I need to start by getting things off my chest, once and for all. I'm ready to air it out. I can't think of a more, as you called it, therapeutic setting." She turned and looked him square in the eye. "You wanted to know my story, so here's your chance."

"Okay."

"I did all the right things growing up. Went to good schools, got a business degree, started a great career and climbed my way to the top. I was so fierce back then. Nobody could stop me. My family provided what they could growing up. We weren't poor, but we always had just enough. Certainly, never an abundance to the degree like my peers had, but that was okay because we had love. My parents always pushed me to be the best and to do better than they did, that way I could go further and live a much better life. God knows how hard I tried. But by thirty-five when I finally took my head out of the sand and looked around me, all my closest friends had already gotten married and even started families. And, where was I? Well, I guess you could say I was on top of the world career-wise, and all alone in every other facet of life. Not exactly a good place to find yourself at that age, or at any time for that matter."

Parker listened intently.

"It was around that time that I met John. In hindsight, there were a lot of warning signs and red flags, but I chose to ignore every one of them. By then I was already determined not to be alone, and he was everything I thought I wanted in a man. It was the perfect match, or so I thought. He was polished, very well accomplished, and just as driven as I was in his career. We were even on the same page with our goals for the future. At least, I thought we were."

Parker shook his head in disbelief, already seeing where this was heading. It was the same old story he'd heard time and time again from his sisters. He swore to his family and to himself that he'd never be that guy, and he hadn't been. All the more reason why he was angry for a long time about losing his forever love.

"I'll bet I can guess how this all plays out. The dirt bag met someone else, deciding that life was too short to be tied down. Maybe even going as far as to say it wasn't you, but it was him who had changed?" he said, sounding disgusted.

"How did you know?"

He picked up a seashell and dusted the sand off. "Sadly, my sisters have had similar experiences. I was around to watch them pick up the pieces before finally meeting the right one."

Meg grunted. "I'm glad they were able to find the right one. That certainly wasn't the case with me."

"Yeah, but that doesn't have to be the way your story ends. I'm sure you already know that, right?"

He watched as a cold stare washed over her face.

"I wouldn't be so sure, Parker. I was way too vulnerable when I met John. I allowed loneliness to weaken my decision making and followed him around for three years. I hoped and I prayed for the day to come when he'd give me his undivided attention... where he'd give me his whole heart instead of loving me half-heartedly. I was such a fool to think I could wait for him to mature." She turned away before she continued speaking. "In a lot of ways, I knew he wasn't the one for me, but chose not to do anything about it out of fear that it was too late to find anyone who would truly love me. How pathetic is that?"

He reached out, touching her shoulder. "Whoa, hold on

there. Don't you think you're being a little harsh on yourself? We all make mistakes. I know I have."

"That's kind of you, Parker. But, when you intentionally choose to stay with a jerk because you think you can't do any better, or you've missed your opportunity, then I'd hardly classify that as a mistake," she explained.

He chuckled, causing Meg to glare at him, therefore he quickly cleaned it up. "I'm sorry. I'm not laughing at your situation. Really, I'm not. It's just — that tough exterior of yours. You're acting like you have your mind made up that falling in love again is completely out of the question. Dare I say that maybe you should consider tearing down your walls of defense," he smiled. "Or maybe that's asking too much from a city girl," he winked, causing her to playfully swing at him and chase him back to the truck.

"Okay, okay. Enough with the jokes on my part. I'm done, I swear," he said, begging for mercy. "Seriously speaking, the guy you were engaged to sounds like the biggest jerk who ever walked the face of planet earth. I'm so sorry you ever had to experience that kind of pain, even for one second. But that doesn't mean there isn't someone out there who wouldn't do anything to get to know you. Who wouldn't do anything to spend time with you, discovering who you are from the inside out, cherishing you, if only you would let them in."

In some ways he was kind of shocked at his level of transparency, but he meant every word of it. Meg had been the first and only woman who captivated his attention in a very long time.

Parker rested on his truck, patting the bumper for her to join him. "The real question is, are you ready to move on and capable of allowing someone in?"

Meg joined him, looking as if she were in deep thought. "I don't know. Most days the idea of entertaining another relationship is a hard no. I mean, let's be clear. I've completely moved on from the idea of ever being with John again. I've been there and I don't want to go down that road ever again. It's probably the wrong way to think, but I'd rather be by myself than ever being hurt like that again."

He knew it was a risk, but there was no time like the present to express what he'd been thinking.

"Where I come from, life's way too short to have regrets and pass up second chances. From the sound of things, you need a man who will value your worth and treat you accordingly. I'd ask a woman like yourself on a date in a heartbeat. You're adventurous, driven, God-fearing, you have a spicy side to your personality, and you're drop dead gorgeous. So much to the point that I had to think twice about being temporary housemates with you. And, I mean that in the most respectful way. All that to say, Meg, you have a lot going for yourself. I hope you never forget it."

Parker removed his keys from his pocket, fully realizing he was making a bold move by admitting what he'd been thinking about her. But, like he said, life was too short to miss out on second chances, and this was one chance he was willing to take. The rest would be up to Meg.

He flipped his keys in the air once, caught them, and when he didn't hear a response from Meg, he began heading toward the driver's door. "It will be getting dark soon and I know you have to get ready for work. We should probably head back to the house."

He sat inside the truck, secretly hoping he hadn't said too much.

Chapter 9

Meg

"Hi, Dad. Yes, everything is fine," Meg explained, knowing her father would have a lot to say about their limited conversation since she arrived.

"Yes, really. Everything is okay. I started my new job, I've unpacked and settled in, and the only thing I'm still working on is —"

She paused on her end of the line, scrambling to think of something other than her reality. Meg knew the minute she revealed to her dad that the beach house plan wasn't all it was cracked up to be, he'd try to rescue her. More than likely scolding her for not saying something sooner, and wiring money that should really be for him and his new bride.

"The only thing I'm still working on is learning my way around. I've been taking a taxi everywhere, but that's getting old very quickly. I'll probably have to hunt for something used or visit a dealer and see if I can find one of those little smart cars to get around in."

She stretched out on a beach chair that was discovered when Miguel began construction. In just a short period of time, his crew had managed to drill the old concrete slab surrounding the pool, remove the tile around the lining, and tear down the surrounding lattice that once created privacy between them and the neighbors.

The construction work didn't really impact her much, given that she still wasn't working from home, and most days she'd return to find the crew was already gone for the day.

Instead, she was usually greeted by the aroma of whatever meal Parker conjured up, ranging anywhere from steaks, to fish, and the occasional take-out he ordered when the workday ran later than planned.

He'd also talked her into morning drop offs at her job a few times a week, something she refused at first. However, it worked out on the days he needed to ride into town for parts and materials. What remained a constant mystery to her was why he was being this nice. Outside of their obvious attraction, and his confession of thinking she was gorgeous, there was really no reason to continue being this nice to somebody he had no real ties to. *Was there?*

"Dad, the seafood here is so fresh, it's amazing. You would absolutely love it. This week I tried some of the Mahi Mahi and it was to die for."

Under normal circumstances she'd invite him to come out and visit, and still planned on doing so, once her new apartment was lined up. By then she needed to have her act together and be ready to explain why she had to move.

"Dad, it's been so good hearing your voice. I miss you guys so much. You have to give Mariam my love, and give her sweet poodle, Sashi, a hug for me, okay?"

Hearing the sound of her dad's voice on the other line touched the depths of her heart, causing her eyes to grow watery. It was the downside to leaving New York, knowing in between visits she was missing out on so much. At least it brought comfort to know he was with someone and happy, unlike herself.

She disconnected the call in time to discover Parker approaching. "There you are. I was starting to wonder if the food I cooked chased you out of the house, or if it was something else," he smiled.

"Oh, no. Dinner was perfect. I just decided to come out here and catch up with my dad, that's all. By the way, you really don't have to include me in your meals. You've been more than generous with the rides to work and our arrangement, really. Cooking for me is way beyond the call of duty."

Parker looked concerned. "It was the food that ran you out of the house, wasn't it?"

Meg gave in to his innocent thinking and his handsome smile. "No, silly. I meant it when I said dinner was perfect. I just don't want you going overboard for me. You have enough going on to keep you busy. If anything, I should be cooking for you." *Did I just say that?*

She hadn't planned on breaking the news to him just yet, but she'd already been eyeing a few apartments, closer to the resort. She'd even had a conversation with Frankie about the rates for renting out a room at the resort, but with the high-end figures she quoted, there was no way. For now, she dedicated a portion of her first check to paying Parker till the end of the month. But she needed to make plans to leave sooner than later. He was becoming too familiar to her; they were falling into a comfortable groove. One she wasn't certain she could handle.

She watched as he made a seat for himself in the sand. "This is starting to become your favorite spot at the beach house, isn't it?" he asked.

"Can you blame me? Every evening it feels like the waves are calling me by name, beckoning for me to come and be one with nature. I figure I might as well enjoy it while I can. At some point, I'll have a regular view when I move closer into town."

He propped his arms on his knees. "About that. You don't have to rush, you know. I was even thinking if you want, I can go down to the dealership with you and help you with hunting for a new car. Of course I'm sure you can handle it just fine on your own, I'm just offering if you'd like an additional presence."

"Uh, thanks. I'm definitely going to need some form of transportation, so I'll let you know." She looked down, noticing a faded beard he was allowing to grow in, making him look even more sexy and rugged than he had up until now.

In true Meg fashion she pushed those thoughts aside and refocused her attention on the water.

Parker cleared his throat. "I was wondering if you were up for another adventure before the sun sets?" he asked.

"I don't know. I might have to pass this time. As it is, I'm supposed to be inside working on a report for my boss on Monday morning."

He gave her a look. "Booo, on a Friday evening? Who does that? I mean, I realize you're still considered new to the team, but surely your boss expects that you would relax on the weekends. It's the only time you have off."

"I know. I just figured if I start now, then the rest of the weekend could be dedicated to other important things, like apartment hunting."

She watched as he picked up a small pebble, tossing it ahead of him, completely ignoring what she just said. "Surely you can spare ten, maybe fifteen minutes tops. This next adventure doesn't even require us to leave the house."

Meg suspiciously sat up, contemplating what the adventure could be. They were living in an old beach house that was in the midst of being renovated. How much adventure could one find in such a place?

"Okay, Mr. King of Adventure, now you have me curious. Give me a minute to get my sandals on and I'll follow you inside. Whatever this is better be really good to take me away from my favorite spot."

Parker stretched his arms to receive help getting up. "Trust me. I think it's something you'll want to see. It's just one more thing to help give you a little –"

"Let me guess, inspiration?" she smiled.

"Well, yeah, what's wrong with being inspired?"

Meg proceeded to pull him up, realizing he was really carrying most of his own weight. As he stood upright, they landed close to one another. Close enough to feel an electrical current run through the pit of her stomach. Close enough to have the desire to kiss him.

She snapped out of it. "Nothing is wrong with it. You're just predictable, that's all. I already knew what you were going to say," she explained as she checked her surroundings and folded the beach chair.

Parker took the chair from her and carried it toward the house. "I don't think anyone has ever told me I'm predictable before. In this case, is that a bad thing, or..."

"Bad? Not at all. It just means I know how to read you a little bit better than I did yesterday, that's all."

The corner of his mouth slowly raised revealing the cutest dimple she'd ever seen. "Okay. Well, since you know how to read me so well, then you should know how excited I am to dive into this little treasure I found," he teased. "Follow me up to the house. We can check it out together."

Meg hoisted her sundress up and buried her feet in the sand, smiling at his take charge demeanor. *Man, oh man. What have you gotten yourself into, Meg Carter?*

* * *

Inside, Meg held a foldable staircase steady as Parker climbed into the attic. "Stay here, I'll be right back," he said.

He didn't have to tell her twice. Dark attic spaces in old houses weren't exactly her cup of tea. Her imagination always ran wild, envisioning some sort of squirrel or random animal jumping out and attacking. All Hollywood, of course, but she still wasn't taking any chances.

"Why are we venturing into the attic, again?" she asked.

Parker yelled down below. "You'll see. Give me one more minute. I just have to crawl to the other side of the beam while trying to avoid the nails at all costs."

"You should be careful. When I was a little girl my father darn near fell right through the attic and landed onto the living room floor. Another time, he managed to fall right down a set of rickety stairs, just like these. Once my mother realized he was okay, she nearly didn't speak to him for a week."

Again, Parker yelled from above, this time sounding further away. "Uh, thanks for the vote of confidence. You're not making me feel nervous about walking around up here at all." She could hear the sound of him sneezing, likely due to the itchy insulation she imagined.

"Gesundheit," she said.

"Thanks. Are you German?"

Meg cocked her head back to see as far into the attic as she possibly could. "No, just a habit I picked up from my great-grandfather. I only know one or two words."

"Got it. So, regarding your dad, how did he manage to fall down the stairs, again?"

Meg giggled to herself at the thought of his obstinance. "He lost his footing on the way down the steps. Lucky for him he was close to the bottom, but that wasn't the first time he'd done something against Mom's wishes. He was always the more stubborn of the two. Mom was the complete opposite."

Parker peered down from the opening of the attic, sliding a large chest near the edge. "I notice you referring to your parents in the past tense. Are either of them still with us?"

"Habit, I guess. Dad's living and has recently remarried. Mom passed several years ago."

She looked up as Parker positioned himself to descend, carefully maneuvering the chest in front of him. "Sorry for your loss. Although I didn't know her, I'm sure your mother would be proud to see you out here reaching your goals," he said.

"Thanks. But, for the record, this ladder looks way too weak for you to be applying weight to it. Is it really necessary to bring that chest down here now?" The crinkled expression across her eyebrows spoke volumes.

"Not to worry. Miguel and I were conducting a walk-through, making a list of other items we would tackle next. Both of us tested the ladder and it's holding up just fine. I promised myself I would come back here later to retrieve the chest and there's no time like the present."

He methodically continued to descend one step, then move the chest down, and repeated the process until he reached the bottom. "See. I made it in one piece. Now, let's bring this baby to the living room and see what's in it."

Meg shook her head, observing the playful, and even boyish side that resided within him. Not exactly the same image she had on the first day they met. Back then Parker was all business, dressed up in a suit and tie, serious, and very matter of fact. As their time together unfolded, he was becoming more adventurous, even more of a true gentleman, thoughtful, and the most challenging of all, more attractive.

She bit her lower lip, trying not to entertain the idea of liking every facet of his personality. But so far, she was losing. Parker Wilson was starting to grow on her.

He kneeled to the floor and opened the chest. "Ah, family

photo albums. That makes sense. Especially for a grandmother who used to host her family here at the beach house." He began flipping through the pages. "This is neat. Here. Why don't you take one, and I'll look through the other. Anything you can find with the name Elizabeth Falcon should be our former owner."

"Sure." She dove in, flipping through the first couple of pages. "I think this is her. The picture is dated over ten years ago with the initials E. F. It looks like she's surrounded by family standing out back by the pool."

* * *

Parker leaned in, admiring the photo. "Wow, she certainly has a large family. Seeing that photo gives me even more of an appreciation for the place. Look at this one," he said, pointing to another photo labeled with Elizabeth's name and the name of a baby she was holding. "This is her for sure."

"She's beautiful. They all are. It's sad they had to let this place go. It seems like they created such great memories here. Just look at them, enjoying one another, the way a family should."

Meg shared a few of the pictures with Parker. "To think of all the special memories they formed here. If only these walls could talk, I'll bet the stories would be endless."

Catching a whiff of his scent was pleasantly intoxicating, causing her to glance his way. Until now, she'd always viewed house flippers as people who wanted to get over. Always looking to make the next quick buck and move on. It was trendy to make everything shine on the surface, but potentially do a botched job, overlooking the things that mattered most. She'd seen it happen so many times. But Parker didn't appear to be that kind of guy. He seemed to care and consider those who would live there.

"Do you think it would be possible to somehow include a tribute to the family in your design? Nothing too personal, but something that honored either the time period they were here, or the original style?"

He blinked, but she couldn't tell what the thought was behind it. "That's a brilliant idea."

A look of curiosity swept across his face. "Have you ever considered getting into property design? I think you'd be pretty good at it."

"Me? Ha, thanks for the compliment, but my expertise lies within hospitality. Even though they always say we have other hidden talents inside of us just waiting to be unleashed."

"All the more reason I can't wait for you to meet my sister tomorrow. I think the two of you together would be a force to be reckoned with. You're both creative. And, you like to think outside of the box. Plus, you're her type."

Meg did a double-take. "Her type?"

"Yeah, the kind of person she'd easily hang out with."

"What type is that?"

Either he was warm, or his face was starting to turn red. "Smart, a good sense of humor, no-nonsense type. You'd easily fit right in around the Wilson family," he explained, shying away toward the end.

"I see." Meg pointed out a few more pictures and also took note of some of the surroundings, displaying the house in its original state. "More than anything, I gather such a sense of love and togetherness from everybody in the pictures. I don't know where her grandkids are today, but it may be worth it for you to try and look them up. I'm sure they would appreciate having a piece of their grandmother's history back in their possession."

Parker perked up. "Not only that, but maybe we can ask a few questions about the house. Get a little background and history before we make any final decisions on the interior design."

She knew she hadn't imagined his glare which appeared to transition back and forth between her eyes and her lips. "We? Sorry, outside of my one or two ideas, you'll have to count me out. I'm going to be buried knee deep in sales and marketing reports for the resort."

"Meg." The mere sound of his voice speaking her name the way he did came across as intimate. She wondered if she was being over the top, imagining things. Or if he was feeling the same level of heat and attraction that occurred between them every time they entered the same room.

"Yes."

"Do you ever think about having children of your own someday? A family to create fun memories with, like the ones we see in these pictures."

She pushed out a long breath and eased back on the couch, sitting alongside him on the floor.

"That's all I ever longed for. To raise children of my own and give them all the experiences in life I never had. And, to love them unconditionally. I wanted it so badly that I allowed myself to fall for the next person I met, instead of trusting my instincts and exercising faith. I ended up right where I am today."

She could feel him turning his shoulders, looking straight at her. "Have you ever considered the idea that the past doors you wanted to remain open were closed for a reason?"

"Well, of course. I just never expected them to be slammed abruptly in my face. But, everything happens for a reason. Clearly the door that included marrying John was shut to protect me from even greater heartache down the line."

"Right. And just as one door closes, it's usually preparation for another wonderful door to be opened. Life doesn't just come to a complete halt because things didn't work out the way you originally planned. There's still time to have a family. There's still time to have it all."

In true Meg fashion she raised her wall of defense. "Nooo. I don't think so."

Before she could explain, Parker's lips were softly engulfing hers, silencing her protest, confirming she wasn't delusional after all. And, to make things more complicated, she didn't pull away.

This is really happening. She heard in her head.

Meg went along for the ride for several minutes, indulging his lips in return, enjoying the embrace of a man once more.

Meg, what are you doing?

She pulled away, recognizing an electrifying current between them, but she still froze just the same. "I have to go."

Without blinking, she ran out, leaving Parker sitting on the living room floor.

Chapter 10

Parker

Parker opened the front door welcoming his sister, Savannah. She stood about five-six in the doorway with her usual crossbody bag and a sketchpad in hand. "Look who finally made it to the front door. I was about two seconds away from turning around and leaving," she said, observing his unkempt appearance.

"Sorry, I guess I overslept."

She took a couple of steps forward, checking out the surroundings. "Oversleeping on a Saturday morning while still in the beginning stages of a new project doesn't sound like you. You sure you're feeling okay?"

He pressed the door closed, inviting her to put her things down. "Hey, there's nothing wrong with getting some extra rest every now and then. Even I need time to recharge," he replied, looking around. "I mean, here we are three weeks into the flip, and we're still working on the exterior. Not exactly the original plan or pace I had in mind."

Savannah ran her hands across the wicker furniture and paused to admire the old chest that was still sitting in the middle of the living room floor. "It's definitely not your usual schedule, but I can't say I'm complaining about it one bit. Making the plan to start construction outdoors bought me the additional time needed to help the kids end the school year and get settled into their summer activities."

"How are the kids doing, by the way? I need to get over to the house and see them soon."

Savannah toured the remainder of the living space, ending up in the kitchen. "They're great. Happy as ever that it's summertime and already at each other's throats over one thing or another. You know, the usual. I'll have to tell them their favorite uncle asked about them."

"What do you mean their favorite uncle? I'm their only uncle," he chuckled.

With every twist and turn around the house, he noticed she appeared to be looking around for someone. "If you're searching for Meg, she's not here."

"Oh, darn. I was really looking forward to meeting her."

He ran both hands through his hair, still trying to make sense of last night. "Yeah, I really wanted you guys to meet, but uh, something tells me that may not happen."

He opened the back door, explaining how he preferred to convert it to something modern made with all glass.

"That's a great idea. I saw something like it recently in a magazine. That idea alone is sure to create a million-dollar view. Your buyers will love it for sure. But, can we back up for a second. What's this hesitation I hear in your voice over your house guest? Anytime we ever check in with one another she's all you ever talk about. Did something happen between you two?"

Parker walked over to the railing and leaned over. "I did something really stupid last night."

Savannah leaned next to him. "Hold that thought. Can I

just steal this house from you and live here myself? Oh my gosh, would you look at the ocean? This, my brother, is by far the best flip you've ever purchased."

They spilled over in laughter, breaking the seriousness in Parker's tone. "Why, thank you. But, unless you're willing to cough up that dollar amount you just quoted earlier, respectfully, the answer is no."

She pushed him gently to the side. "Wow, okay, I see how you are," she teased. "Seriously, what's the deal with this girl? I haven't seen you act like this since –"

"Go ahead, you can say her name. Since Jenna?"

Savannah nodded. "Well, yeah. And, to be honest, I'm quite surprised. You haven't said much about anybody in a very long time. I think the last time you tried to go on a date you ended up getting cold feet. The poor woman is still probably talking badly about you to this day."

"Savannah, you play too much. That's not how it went at all. A friend set me up on a blind date, and since that's not really my thing, I didn't want to go through with it. I was uncomfortable with the idea, but I didn't back out. She's the one who canceled on me," he explained.

"Alright, alright. Don't get your undies in a bunch. The point is you haven't been interested in anyone until now, so I want to know, what's changed? It's not every day that you take in a strange woman to live in one of your flips, Park."

"True. But I don't know what to tell you. I can't explain it other than to say, Meg is no ordinary woman."

Savannah drew her head back, holding a look of surprise. "Oooh, now I really want to meet this woman. What did you do to run her out of here so quickly?"

"Surely you came over here to start jotting down a few tile ideas for the bathrooms."

Savannah pulled up a chair and made herself comfortable.

"Hey, you're the one who started the conversation. Don't get upset with me for trying to finish it. Now, what happened?"

He held down his head. "I kissed her. In hindsight, it was probably too soon. We were sitting around looking at old photo albums of the family that used to live here, and we got to talking, and I don't know. I sensed an attraction between us, and I thought maybe she felt it too. From the moment I discovered her standing out here, she captivated my attention. I think everything about her is beautiful and perfect in every way, and I suppose I got caught up, allowing my feelings to get the best of me."

Savannah chuckled out loud. "Did she haul off and smack you?"

"Savannah Jeffries, that's a terrible thing to say. Of course not. I was still respectful. What kind of man do you think I am?"

"You know I'm teasing. Although, I'm sure you caught her off guard. How did she react, before you ran her out of the house?"

He could tell she was having way too much fun with this, but the banter was all a part of their playful nature. With her being the not so typical middle child, and him being the youngest, that hadn't changed much over the years.

"Actually, she kissed me back. It felt amazing, Van. Just like I imagined it would. Look, I don't know if I'm making more of it than I should. I'm so out of practice when it comes to this kind of stuff, until it's pathetic. One minute I'm at the closing, signing on the dotted line, and the next I come here to find the most stunning woman I've ever met since Jenna passed." He took a moment to process everything he was feeling toward Meg.

"To be clear. If it were just her beauty, I'd overlook it. Beautiful women are everywhere. That's not it. It's who she is as a person that speaks to me. She came here in a matter of no time and snatched me right out of this coma I've been under for the last three years. I actually feel alive again, and excited to wake up and see her every day."

Savannah began clapping slowly and gave Parker a standing ovation, leaving him confused.

"What's that for?" he asked.

She approached him with open arms. "I'm applauding my little brother for allowing himself to feel again. I'm proud of you, Parker." After a long hug she propped her arm on his shoulder. "You know what else?"

"What?" he asked.

"Good on you for being brave enough to make the first move. Trust me when I tell you, the woman likes you just as much as you like her. If she found you to be even the least bit repulsive, she wouldn't have kissed you back."

Parker flipped his sister over his shoulder pretending to run her down to the ocean water to throw her in. "That does it. That will be the last time I tell you anything."

"Alright, alright. I'll stop teasing you," she surrendered. "All jokes aside, if her belongings are still here, she'll be back. At that time, you can sit her down and tell her you didn't mean to do anything to make her uncomfortable. And, if you think the time is right, tell her everything you just told me. Women like hearing a man's inner thoughts."

He wasn't so sure about that. As it was, his bravery to make the first move had already gotten him in a heap of trouble. The last thing Meg probably wanted to hear was a true confession of feelings. He'd probably sound like some desperate loser who hadn't dated in ages. That alone would probably be a turn off.

"I don't know, sis. You've always been one to give me good advice, but I'm not so sure this time."

She smiled. "Have I ever failed you? I've only been married

twelve years; therefore, I may have a little bit more experience under my belt. Besides, who's to say she ran off because of you. Maybe she's facing her own internal fears, something the both of you have in common."

* * *

Back inside, they continued talking before transitioning to their original reason for meeting. Savannah removed a couple of kitchen backsplash samples from her satchel and lined them up along the counter. "I was thinking about going with glass tiles for the backsplash, maybe in a subtle blue or deep Sahara color to tie in the colors of the beach. That in conjunction with the white cabinets we talked about would look very nice. What do you think?"

He nodded. "It meets my approval. It also falls in line with some of the modern flips I've seen in the area."

"Perfect. Now, just like in our other flips, I want to be careful to incorporate the true feeling of living in a Bahamian beach house. If we go too crazy with all the modern touches, I'm afraid we'll lose that tropical oasis vibe we're going for."

"Agreed."

In the background Parker heard the sound of a car door slamming shut. With the twist of a few keys, Meg entered.

Savannah mouthed the words *I told you she'd be back.* But it was all he could do to get himself together, straightening out his jeans and white t-shirt, making himself look as presentable as possible.

"Meg, is that you?" He called out.

"Hey, Parker, don't mind me. Just stopped by to grab a few things."

He raised his hands and folded his eyebrows at Savannah, in confusion.

To which Savannah replied by whispering, "go talk to her."

This was ridiculous in his opinion. A grown man breaking out into a sweat, having to take coaching lessons from his sister about how to approach his crush. At forty years old, one would think he'd have it together by now.

"Uh, if you have a minute, I'd like to introduce you to my sister, Savannah. We're back here in the kitchen."

Meg popped her head in, subtly waving. "Hi, I'm Meg. It's nice to meet you."

Parker listened as his sister gave her a warm welcome in return. "It's nice to meet you. I've heard so much about you," she said.

Ugh, really Savannah? he thought, but allowed her to carry on. He noticed Meg's sundress and semi-wet curls, which made him curious about where she'd been. He also noticed her t-strap sandals, red toenail polish, and for the first time ever, a tan line on her ring finger, marking the place where her engagement ring once rested.

Meg clutched the strap to her purse. "It was nice meeting you, but I certainly don't want to get in your way. I'm sure you two have a lot of planning to do."

Savannah checked her cell phone. "Your timing couldn't be more perfect. We're pretty much done talking about the backsplash and tile for now. Our next meeting will be at the warehouse where we have to pick out kitchen cabinet samples, isn't that right, Parker?" she winked.

He caught on quickly, recognizing that as her potential exit strategy.

"Yes, the warehouse should be our next stop, for sure. How about you text me later on this week and let me know what day works for you? Maybe by then we'll have a couple of ideas in mind for the flooring as well."

Savannah slipped by Meg. "That sounds perfect." She then

checked the time. "Ooh, if I get a move on, I think I can squeeze in a pedicure before it's time to relieve my sitter. Love you, Parks. Nice meeting you again, Meg!" she yelled from the front door, then closed it behind her.

* * *

The two of them were left standing in the kitchen glaring at first into each other's eyes, then in different directions, trying at all costs to avoid feeling awkward.

"Meg."

"Parker."

They laughed.

"Please, allow me to go first," he said.

"Sure."

He inhaled, followed by a long release of air, allowing himself time to think straight.

"I owe you an apology."

Meg nervously waved him off. "Don't be silly. We both played an active role, but it was nothing, really."

Feeling taken back by her comment, he paused, then continued. "That's an interesting choice of words. It certainly didn't feel like nothing."

"Parker, I don't mean anything by it, but what did we expect?" She lifted her hand toward the backdrop of the ocean. "Two single adults, sharing a house together in such a romantic setting. Neither of us are in a relationship, and—well, sometimes these things happen. It doesn't mean there's anything behind it."

"Interesting. The only problem is I'm not that kind of guy. I don't just sit back and allow these kinds of things to happen. Heck, normally I wouldn't allow anyone to be living here, period. So, I'm definitely acting out of character. Speaking of which, I know you're independent and don't have to answer to me, but I was worried about you last night. Where did you go?"

She placed her purse down on the counter and folded her arms. "To my office at the resort. I figured if I brought a few things and pulled an all-nighter, then I could knock the reports out of the way and have the remainder of the weekend to relax. It would've been a successful plan if I didn't have to sit up in a chair all night. I'm sure my backside will be sore for days."

They laughed, temporarily cutting the tension, but he sensed there was more on her mind.

"I'm glad you were able to get some work done. But next time it sure would be nice for you to let a guy know that you're okay. I didn't hardly get any sleep, thinking about where you could possibly be."

In that moment, he remembered his sister's words about sharing his heart. "Meg, if I made you uncomfortable last night, I'm sorry. But I can't sit here and pretend that I didn't like it. If you allow me, I wouldn't hesitate to kiss you all over again. I'm attracted to you, Meg. I'm drawn to your fire-like personality, your strength. Most importantly, your ability to pick up the pieces and move on with life, even after going through something so difficult. Maybe it's a little soon for me to be telling you these things, I don't know. But after spending the last few weeks with you, somehow, I think you feel it too."

"Parker –" she said, looking confused.

"No, please allow me to finish. I'm not sure where all of this is heading. But I know that I'm into you. Those words haven't been vocalized to anyone since my fiancé. There's something about you that makes me feel alive again, and I don't want to hide those feelings anymore."

Meg reached to open her purse, pulling out a white envelope and handing it over to him. She took a deep breath and with partially watery eyes said, "here. This is for you. It's the money I owe you for my room and board, plus a little extra as my way of saying thank you."

He felt as if time and everything else around him came to a halt. If he weren't standing there frozen and numb, maybe he'd have the courage to repeat himself. Maybe she didn't hear him clearly the first time.

Finally, the words escaped. "Meg, please don't do this."

"What do you mean don't do this?" she smiled. "I have to pay you. Plus, we both went into this knowing it was temporary."

He dropped the envelope on the counter. "Then why does this conversation sound so conclusive, like you're about to pack everything and leave this weekend?"

"It's because I am. I'm trying to be as sensitive as I possibly can be, but I can no longer stay here with you. I arrived here one month after being kicked to the curb by the man I was supposed to marry. Somehow, I don't think I'm qualified to fall for another man in such a short period of time. It's too soon."

She turned away. "One of my co-workers has an extra room at her place. It's probably best that I stay with her. Besides, you're in the process of trying to renovate a house. The sooner I get out of your way, the better."

And just like that, Parker received what felt like a final blow to the stomach leaving him winded. Maybe it was a final blow to his ego. Either way, it hurt.

So much for stepping out on a limb and following his heart. So much for opening up and trying to love again. Perhaps the safest place for him to dwell would be in his own cocoon where he could remain alone.

Chapter 11

Meg

With boxes stacked a mile high in her room, Meg was no closer to being settled than the day she landed in the Bahamas. Frankie had been generous to offer her a place to stay at a discounted rate. However, all of her belongings stacked in an eleven-by-eleven room couldn't last forever.

"Frankie, thank you for opening up your home to me. I promise you won't even know that I'm here."

"Oh, Meg, please. I know we're co-workers, but you're someone I can officially call a friend. And, as my friend, there's no need to tip-toe around here as if you don't belong. Mi casa su casa. Comprende?"

Meg let out a hearty chuckle. "Si. I didn't realize you were fluent in Spanish."

"I picked up a couple of words in middle school, but that's about it. I can't hold a sentence to save my life. But seriously, I want you to be comfortable. I have a spare closet upstairs and a small shed out back in case you want to use it for storage."

"Thank you, Frankie."

Frankie tilted her head, checking on Meg as if she were sick. "You miss him, don't you?"

Was it that obvious?

Meg knew she'd been distracted, but maybe she was wearing her feelings on her sleeve, publicly broadcasting her feelings for Parker a little bit more than she had intended.

"No. Miss him? I'm fine," she replied.

"Mm hmm. You may think you're fine, but something tells me you're not being honest with yourself. Who in their right mind spends a Friday night working at the resort, then turns around and moves all in the same weekend? No one that I know, that's for sure."

Meg smirked and nodded in agreement. "Okay, so I was a little overzealous this weekend. I just wanted to hurry up and get settled already. Bouncing around from place to place may work for some, but it certainly doesn't work for me."

"I get it. But, please humor me if you will."

"Okay," Meg smiled.

"Unbeknownst to anyone except for your best friend back home, you relocate here and move in with a guy you hardly know."

Frankie was going straight to the heart of the matter, describing her situation to a tee. Unfortunately, she didn't recognize the woman she was describing. Normally, Meg wouldn't do such a thing. But she hadn't felt normal in a while. She hadn't been herself since the day her ex broke things off. What made her think moving to a distant island would change anything?

"Yep, that pretty much sums things up," Meg said.

"No, it doesn't. I recognize that gaze in your eyes. You haven't been able to concentrate for long without daydreaming or getting lost in that pretty head of yours. Whoever this man is, he did a real number on you. You may have stayed initially for room and board, but what you found at that beach house was love."

"Frankie, what on earth are you talking about?"

She pointed at Meg. "You can play innocent if you like, but you know exactly where I'm going with this. You're hooked on Mr. Beach House Flip. You just don't want to admit it."

After a moment of sitting in silence without agreeing to, or denying the claim, Meg watched as Frankie held her hands up.

"Look, how about we put that conversation to the side for now? I have an idea. These boxes can wait until later on. You can always knock out some of the unpacking tomorrow since you're working from home. While the day is still young, let's do a little exploring, shall we? We can take a ferry ride over to Paradise Island and visit Atlantis. It will be a fun way to relax and take your mind off things. Have you ever been to the Island?"

"No, I've heard about it on commercials, and I've seen brochures, but I've never been. But, Frankie, you don't have to do this for me. It's my goal to stay out of your hair, not giving you something extra to do," Meg replied.

"Girl, I need the break just as much as you do. Plus, it will give me a chance to learn more about your new lover boy."

Meg pretended to toss an old t-shirt her way. "You are so ridiculous, Frankie!" she laughed.

"Ridiculous or not I'll meet you in the driveway in fifteen minutes. Oh, and be sure to wear a bathing suit. I have passes to get us on the grounds so we can enjoy their facilities."

* * *

A breezy ferry ride surrounded by blue ocean water was just what Meg needed to help clear her mind. With her arms outstretched, taking in the sun, Meg's skin was taking on a more permanent tan. Something she could get used to.

Her new look blended beautifully with the coral and light-colored clothing she packed. To think, just a year ago she needed the assistance of a tanning salon to achieve such a look.

"Oh my goodness, Frankie. It's absolutely stunning out here. Would you look at this? No honking sounds from taxi cab drivers, no smog, no hustle and bustle. Just crystal-clear water, a relaxing breeze, and pure paradise," she said, closing her eyes.

"I know, hun. It's the very reason I ended up staying. Don't get me wrong, I miss being around my family. But, living in the Bahamas was a natural fit for me. I knew it from the moment I set foot on the island. Even though it wasn't my original reason for coming."

Meg slid a pair of sunglasses over her eyes. "I think it's wonderful that you were able to find happiness, even if it wasn't in the form of a relationship. That's what I want for myself actually. And, now that I made the move, I can see myself achieving it. No men, no heartaches, no distractions. Just a peaceful... single... life. That's all I want."

"Ha! That's a good one. Very funny, Meg. Verrry funny!"

"What? I'm not trying to be funny. If anything, I am more serious now than ever."

Frankie rolled her eyes. "Uh huh, sure you are."

Meg threw a dagger Frankie's way underneath the layer of her sunglasses which went undetected. "I have a track record that speaks for itself. My dating history is filled with nothing but one failed attempt after another. This last one was the icing on the cake."

"Mm hmm."

"Seriously, Frankie, I gave up everything for my ex. Everything! And, what did I get in return? Nothing but a nervous smile as he revealed that he was in a relationship with someone else— and this was while we were at a cake tasting, no less."

Frankie slowly began clapping, then picked up the tempo to a full applause, causing Meg to look around. "You know what I have to say to that? Bravo! Bravo for actually making it through such a rotten experience. You survived. And, not only did you survive but you're still standing on your own two feet, chasing after your dreams. That I can embrace. But, why you would ever want to declare living single for the rest of your life is beyond me."

A gentleman standing at the front of the boat cleared his throat and began announcing, "Good afternoon, ladies and gentleman, boys and girls. Welcome to the beautiful islands of the Bahamas. In the next ten minutes we will be approaching Paradise Island. Hold on to your hats and prepare to visit one of the most popular ports in the Bahamas, formerly known as Hog Island. Over to your right —"

Meg leaned over. "I don't see how I'm doing anything wrong. You can't continually be stepped on like a doormat and not expect to finally decide to take a different course of action. It's called learning how to wise up, that's all. Besides, how are you going to give me a lecture about being single when you're not dating either? It doesn't make any sense."

"Correction. I'm not dating because I haven't met anyone. However, what I'm not doing is completely closing myself off if the opportunity presents itself. You, my dear, have an opportunity. And, your way of embracing it, which in essence is slamming the door to the idea altogether. Big difference, don't you think?"

Meg grunted. "We're missing our tour guide's speech."

"You're missing out, alright. But, it's not on a speech."

* * *

Meg's tube float bobbed and weaved behind Frankie's as they glided along the wave pool at Atlantis Resort. It was hard to believe in less than twenty-four hours she'd have to log in and report to work. Her new tropical life was starting to drown out her past, and she didn't see any reason why that needed to end.

"Frankie, you're a godsend. What was supposed to be a bad weekend was quickly transformed into a mini vacation. Apparently, something I needed."

"Oh, no problem, darlin. I have only one special request to make before we get ready to head back to the ferry."

"Sure, whatcha got?"

Meg's eyes followed as Frankie pointed up to the tallest water slide the resort had to offer. She could faintly hear screams as each individual took the deep plunge. "Uh, negative! No, thanks. I was game to take to the ferry ride over here, even to try some new food. But I don't do water slides — this calm wave pool is as crazy as it gets."

"Come on, Meg. Don't be a chicken. Try it once and if you really don't like it, then you never have to do it again."

"Ha! I'm not falling for it. That's what they all say. But the minute somebody finds themselves paralyzed after plunging, more like slapping down into the deep abyss, then all the fun and games are over."

Frankie began tugging on Meg's floating tube. "Oh, stop being dramatic. There are no such reports. It's all a figment of your imagination."

"Mm, okay. Well, I guess I'll be a chicken then. At least chickens know how to play it safe."

"My point exactly," Frankie replied.

Meg gave her a side-eye. "What point?"

"Pretend for one moment that slide is your exit ticket to get away from everything that's holding you back."

"Um, I believe most people would view that as a joy ride, maybe even a death wish, but nothing more."

"Work with me here. You want to be free, don't you? You want a fresh start, so much so that you packed your bags and moved all the way out here, didn't you?" Frankie emphasized.

"Well, yeah, but — "

"No buts! I don't need to go on the water slide. I've been on it several times since I moved out here. But I'll tell you one thing. Every single time I close my eyes and let go, it is the most freeing and exhilarating feeling I've ever experienced in my life. And, I'm still in one piece," Frankie said, beating her chest.

"Good grief. You are such a nut job!" Meg giggled.

"An honest nut job. I wouldn't lie to you, and I wouldn't lead you astray, Meg. I recognize what you're going through right now because at one point I was in your shoes. The real reason I brought you on this little excursion today is because you need to learn to let go, so you can live your best life, for goodness' sake."

As they drew near to the end of the wave pool, Frankie continued pressing the matter.

"Your new beach house guy may or may not be the right one for you, but you'll never know until you allow yourself to be free and stop living according to all these restrictions you've concocted in your head."

"So, what? Just throw all caution to the wind? I'm sorry, that's not how I was raised. Up until recently I used to lean on faith to determine my outcomes, but after all those years of being hopeful, if this is the hand I've been dealt, then so be it. I can live with that," Meg replied.

"No, my dear. That's not how it works. Nobody is telling you to stop being hopeful. But what I am saying is don't neglect every single day that God gives you to get out there and live. That's all. It's a huge leap, I get it. It can be scary at times. But, get out there and conquer it anyway. Get up every single day and be ready to take the plunge. And, if you fail, who cares? Get up and try again the next day. It's way better than closing yourself off and potentially missing out on another chance at love."

Meg allowed her words to marinate as they toweled off. She slid into her flip flops and strolled to a nearby row of beach chairs to gather their belongings. "Hmm, and what's this whole slide experience supposed to do for me again? I mean, outside of darn near giving me a heart attack and all."

Frankie cracked up. "It's teaching you how to stop trying to have so much control over everything and be free to have fun and enjoy life."

Meg assessed the height of the slide. "How tall is it again?"

"Meg!"

"Okay, okay. I just wanted to know what we were working with, that's all."

"No, I didn't go down the slide! Casey, you know me better than that. I took one step forward, thought about it, then turned around and left." Meg howled with laughter while fully submerged in bath bubbles.

"That's too bad. I'm with your friend, Frankie, on this one. There's no harm in stepping out on a limb and trying something new, Meg. Even if that something new seems kind of scary at first."

Meg blew the bubbles in front of her out of the way. "I know, and while I completely understand where she was going with the whole slide analogy, I'm just not sure that I'm ready yet."

"Not ready for the slide? Or not ready to let go of your past?"

Meg didn't have to think long about it. The writing was

clear on the wall. John was history. But the fear of being hurt and deeply disappointed was still very real.

"Both! But as it pertains to love, somewhere along the line I managed to put up a ton of guard rails to protect myself. I'm not sure when it happened. But my guard rails feel safe, and I don't see myself taking them down anytime soon."

The sound of screaming children interrupted her thought pattern.

"Hold on a second, Meg. I'll be right back."

Meg twirled her toes around in the soap suds, envisioning the relationship she was involved in prior to the one with John. It was another long-term commitment, dedicated to one man. Her heart was always loyal to one and that hadn't wavered. Except, unlike John, he didn't struggle with infidelity. He was just an unhealthy problem with over indulging in his quest to become an entrepreneur, always putting their time together on the back-burner.

"Okay, are you still there?" Casey asked.

"Yep, I'm here. Just soaking in the tub, turning into quite the raisin I might add."

"Ha, can we trade places? I'd give anything to have just a half hour of uninterrupted time to take a peaceful bath. If only my kids could manage without trying to half kill each other!"

Meg chuckled. "Oh, dear. The next time I'm in town I'll have to come over and give you some relief."

"I can book you on the next flight if you'd like. Just say the word." They laughed.

The idea sounded tempting to Meg, but she knew the island was where she needed to be. "How about Christmas time?"

"Sure, but until then, I have a little challenge of my own for you to work on. If you don't want to try the slide for now... fine. Although I have to admit that I'm totally jealous that my dream vacation is right at your fingertips and you won't take full advantage of it."

"Heyyy, that's not true. I'm all for the beach and even the wave pool, but the slide – that's another story," Meg replied.

"Okay, well, skip the slide for now. But, do me a favor. Prove to yourself that you still have what it takes to get back out there again. If you felt electricity between you and Parker, call him up and ask him out on a date. He already made the first move, so now it's your turn. At minimum, tell him you were thinking about him. It's not like you would be lying. Would you?"

Meg held the phone well away from her ear and pretended to scream at the top of her lungs. After taking a deep breath she returned to the conversation. "If I didn't know any better, I'd think you and Frankie were related."

"Who knows. Maybe we're sisters from another lifetime. Either way, next time we talk, I want to hear that you called the man already. Now, before we go, how's your new job coming along? Are you well on your way to becoming the resort's top saleswoman of the year?"

Meg leaned her head against the wall of the tub, letting out a long sigh. "I'm trying. Not so sure that goal would be realistic for my first year, but I'm definitely trying to make strides."

"Atta girl. I love you, Meg, and hopefully it goes without saying that I miss you tons."

"I love you and miss you too, friend."

"Say hello to your dad for me," Casey expressed.

"Will do, he's next on my list of phone calls. I'll be sure to relay the message. Please hug the kids and say hello to Craig for me."

"I sure will. Oh, and, Meg?"

"Yes?"

"You are going to call him, aren't you?" Casey said, lowering her voice.

"Casey! Are you there? I think there's a little static on the line... shhhh.... shhhh... we're breaking up."

"Meg Carter! I know what you're doing. I'll get you back for this!"

"Shhh, shhhhh," she continued to tease, and then disconnected the line.

Chapter 12

Parker

Parker removed the last wooden panel off the wall, working alongside Miguel and his crew. The pool held them up for a while. But now the kitchen demolition was complete, with all the cabinets and appliances removed. They were standing in front of a clean slate, awaiting Parker's fresh vision.

"Great work, guys. With the demo behind us, I feel like we can start to make some real headway. I have my cabinet guy working on a custom design that should be ready for install in two weeks. In the meantime, we need to get these walls painted and the flooring that my sister picked out installed. Let's hope and pray we don't run into any issues along the way."

Miguel nodded. "Sounds like a plan, boss. We'll have this kitchen looking good in no time. For now, we're going to get the trash in the dump for you and then head out for the day."

"Thanks, Miguel."

The sound of a basketball bouncing caught Parker's attention, growing increasingly louder. Through the front shutters he could see the neighbors' kids playing in the driveway. A habit he gladly welcomed as long as they didn't get in the way. He'd found the hoop resting on the side of the house and decided to put it to good use. Making it a great stress reliever on days when the reno wasn't going according to plan.

This particular afternoon as they played, he noticed a car rolling up the driveway behind them.

"Miguel, I'll be out front if you guys need me," he called.

"Yes, boss, no problem!"

Parker stepped onto the front porch, raising his hand above his eyebrows, blocking out the sun. "Watch your back, fellas. A car is coming up."

With the glare making it difficult to see, it wasn't until the door opened that he spotted those recognizable legs emerging. At that point, he knew it was his former housemate, Meg.

She stepped out of the car and waved. "Hey, Parker."

Was it normal that she was still having an impact on his heart, making it race? He wondered.

After all, he didn't expect to hear from Meg again. Especially with the way she'd packed up and exited so quickly. On the flip side, had she really done anything wrong? Technically, no. Nothing outside of crushing his ego, which he could recover from. Besides, as they'd stated earlier, their arrangement was always supposed to be temporary. If he stuck with that line of thinking, everything would be fine. Right?

"Meg, didn't expect to see you here," he replied. Then, he directed his attention to the neighbor's kids. "Meet Anton and Camilo. They live two doors down."

"Anton and Camilo, it's nice to meet you. My name is Meg."

The boys reached for Meg's hand, then giggled and gave Parker a look of approval.

"Alright, you two. Miguel and his crew are going to start dumping a lot of old wooden cabinets and I don't want you to get hurt. What do you say we squeeze in a quick game tomorrow evening? Maybe this old man can teach you a thing or two."

"Okay, Mr. Parker," Camilo answered on behalf of his brother. Then the two ran off. "Bye, Miss Meg!" one called back.

"It was nice meeting you!"

As she returned her attention to Parker, their eyes locked. That's when it all came back to him. That electrifying current that drew him in whenever he looked into her eyes.

"How are you?" he asked.

"I'm doing well. Finally settling in and--" She pointed to the shiny car in the driveway. "I went ahead and picked up a new vehicle this morning. Keeping up with the cab fees was starting to get kind of old."

He strolled over and circled around the perimeter of the vehicle. "Nice! It looks like it's in great shape. Is it new?"

"It's new to me. The mileage is pretty low, and my mechanic gave it the seal of approval. Overall, I'm happy with the purchase. Now I just have to get used to driving on the left side of the road," she chuckled.

He slid his hand over the top of the car. "I'm sure you'll get the hang of it in no time."

After a couple of minutes of small talk, he wondered what led her to stop by. Surely it wasn't to show off her car. Meg wasn't that kind of woman.

"I can almost bet you're not looking for another place to rent," he teased. "What brings you by today?"

She took a deep breath, while flattening out the pleats in her dress. "You." She corrected herself. "I mean, I came by because I needed to talk to you. The way I left things between us wasn't exactly one of my best moments. I should've been more –"

"Meg. There's no need to explain. I was pretty foolish to

think anything would come of it," he said, picking up the basketball. "Let's be real. The only reason why we're even aware of the other's existence is because of a misunderstanding. The whole thing is my fault. I got ahead of myself."

"Parker, please hear me out. How we came together doesn't matter. All that matters is how we feel about each other."

That comment was a stretch in his opinion. The way he saw it, he was the one with all the feelings, and she was the one who hightailed it to dodge a bullet.

"Feelings?" he asked.

"Yes." She reached out her hand and grazed his. "Listen, you know my fears. I'd be lying if I didn't say I'm still a little raw right now, maybe even afraid. But that doesn't mean I don't have feelings for you. What we shared the night that you kissed me—" Her voice trailed off into a whisper in the end. "I want to experience that again."

Instead of taking her by the hand, he gazed beyond her. "Yeah, well, I have issues of my own to deal with, but that didn't stop me from taking a chance that night. One of those issues you exposed early on."

He watched as she retreated a bit. "What do you mean?"

"Living this nomadic life as you refer to it is a way to make a living, but it's also my way of dealing with loss, and dodging the idea of making lasting connections. At least, that's what my therapist used to tell me."

Meg's eyebrows folded. "How so?"

"According to her, I never get attached to anything for too long. I move in, get the job done, and then I move on. I recognize a few faces in the community, but I never have to stick with one neighborhood too long to care. I never have to attend any community gatherings, never have to make any attempts to build long-lasting relationships. Except for the one with my sister, but that doesn't count.

"I'm so good at living an isolated life until it comes naturally, just like breathing."

Meg tucked a few strands of hair behind her ear, letting out a nervous chuckle. "Parker, don't you think you're being a little hard on yourself? I mean, if you didn't care to build a relationship with anybody, how did you allow yourself to be so free with me?"

The thunderous sound of cabinets dropping into a dumpster interrupted them.

Parker looked back. "Sorry about the noise. The guys are almost done wrapping things up."

He scooped up the ball, bouncing it a few times, then tossed it over to the side. "As for your question, I really don't know what to say. You caught me off guard, sparking something different in me that I hadn't felt before. But, the real Parker Wilson, he always finds a way to avoid getting deeply invested. He knows how to walk the fine line of being friendly, but not getting too deeply involved. It's his protective layer. So, in a lot of ways, I guess you dodged a bullet by moving out when you did."

The stare she gave him looked like one of disbelief, or maybe even sheer confusion. He'd hoped she'd buy into what he was saying. Not that he was lying. It was true that he'd been playing it pretty safe since Jenna's death, keeping to himself. But it's not like he was doing it to be a malicious heartbreaker or anything. In his mind maybe if she viewed him as a risk, she'd back off, and he wouldn't have to confront his newfound feelings. After all, taking a chance on love always had the potential of coming with risk.

Meg folded her arms. "I don't believe you. Sure, you might have hang ups just like anyone who's ever had their heart broken. But you're a good guy, Parker. Plus, I felt something that night — we both did. It was so real that even I got scared and ran."

He quickly retorted back. "So, what's changed? It hasn't been that long since you left. Now all of a sudden you want to be a risk taker?"

Meg released her arms to her side. "Kiss me again."

"What?" he said, looking around as if he'd heard wrong.

"I said, kiss me again. If nothing else, we ought to prove to ourselves that we don't have to remain stuck in the past for the rest of our lives. Go ahead and kiss me again."

"Meg."

She cupped his cheeks with both hands and planted a long, sultry kiss on his mouth, making it difficult to refuse. He gave in, placing the palm of his hands on the warmth of her back, returning one deep kiss with another until he snapped.

Pulling back was the last thing he wanted to do, but he had to.

"Meg, this isn't a game to me. My feelings for you are just as real as my reservations about my past. I have no idea what I'm capable or incapable of. I'm not even sure I know how to love again. But the one thing I know right now is true -– it's probably a safer bet to quit while we're ahead."

"So, you're really going to choose to recoil back to your old self instead of pressing beyond your fears?"

He gently raised the top of her hand to his mouth, giving her a soft peck. With frustration reverberating through his body, he was left torn between walking away or grabbing her into his arms.

Nevertheless, he backed away, with his mind tugging him in one direction and his heart pulling him in another.

"I'm sorry."

Chapter 13

Frankie

Frankie could see Meg's waning energy as she pretended to be fine at work. A week had passed since Meg's conversation with Parker. And the only thing she could visibly see was her roommate acting withdrawn. Maybe even putting up a protective wall as a defense mechanism. She wasn't sure. Outside of sharing what happened, Meg hadn't said much about Parker. She hadn't said much about anything at all.

"Knock-knock," Frankie grinned, peering her head into Meg's office.

"Hi, Frankie."

"Good afternoon. I came to check and see if you are willing to pull your head out of the sand for a little while."

"Pull my head out of the sand? Ha! There's no such thing. I have to squeeze in as much as I can because tomorrow is my work from home day. You know what that means. Non-stop Zoom meetings."

"Yes, however, I'm not sure if you noticed, but it's time to eat. I'm grabbing a bite with my friend, Margaret, down at the Stoned Crab. Why don't you join us?"

Meg slouched back in her swivel chair, offering a lazy smile. "Thanks for thinking of me, but –"

"Nope. Don't do it. I'm not accepting any excuses. You've been living in an isolated bubble for over a week now. It's time for you to break out of these four walls and talk about it over some shrimp and grits," Frankie argued.

"Shrimp mixed with grits, on the same plate?"

"Oh, you don't know what you're missing. If that doesn't do it for you, they have Frittatas, seafood fettuccini, grilled scallops, you name it. You'll come back with a doggy bag and enough food in your belly to put you into a coma!" Frankie laughed. "Come on, Meg, give yourself a break."

Delivering a sandwich to her desk was always an option. But what better way to help her roomie recharge than to remove her from the premises for a while. Smelling the fresh air and taking in the ocean view could make all the difference in her day. Plus, if there was any chance, she could potentially get Meg to talk, that would be even better.

Meg glanced at the digital clock that read noon. "I have an important call to take at two, so I'll need to be back before then. I guess an hour lunch won't hurt. But not one minute beyond, Frankie, I mean it."

"One hour. Got it."

* * *

Within a ten-minute ride downtown, Frankie pulled into a side street to park. "Margaret just texted to say her meeting ran late. She wants us to go ahead and get started without her."

"That stinks, but I can completely relate. Some days it's so slammed I barely have time to eat -- How did you two meet again?" Meg asked.

"At the resort. She actually used to be in my position, and she trained me before leaving. She works over at the Grand Isle Resort now."

"Ooh, okay. Fancy."

"Ha! I think we're a tough competitor at The Cove, don't you think?" Frankie asked.

"We're not far off. But Grand Isle was definitely a resort I considered when sending out my resume."

When they arrived, Frankie tossed her heels in the trunk, trading them for slide-on sandals and a pair of sunglasses.

"See, Frankie, that's what I like about you. You are always prepared. I need to think about these kinds of things."

"Honey, I learned very quickly that in order to survive on this island, you need some comfortable walking shoes. I could go on for days about all the damage I've done to these feet of mine while trying to be cute. I went from wearing a four-inch heel, to a three-inch, down to a 1-inch pump. Not the sexiest option in the closet, but my feet are forever grateful," Frankie cackled just thinking about all the dumb things she used to do in the name of trying to be cute. Wearing high heels being one of them.

"More power to all the women out there who can successfully wear four-inch heels without developing hammer toes."

"Hammer toes?" Meg busted into laughter.

"I'm just saying! Anyway, we didn't come here to talk about fashion. I want to know what's going on with you these days. Somebody has been awfully quiet lately. And it sure the heck isn't me!"

Meg smiled at the host, then followed her past the sound of clinking glasses and utensils. "Frankie, when you said lunch, you weren't messing around. This place looks like it easily gets five-stars, and four-dollar signs in the Zagat restaurant guide," she whispered.

Frankie chuckled, inhaling the scent of shrimp scampi on their way to their seats. "It may be, but a girl has the right to treat herself every now and again. Who's to say you have to wait around for a man to take you on a date in order to enjoy a nice restaurant?"

Meg groaned. "Agreed."

Frankie positioned herself comfortably on the plush leather seating and secured an additional setting for Margaret. "Now, once again. Are you going to tell me why you've been so quiet lately? Or am I going to have to drag it out of you?"

"Frankie, I don't want every outing to be about me. Plus, your friend is coming, and I don't want to burden her with my –"

"Eh-eh. Don't go there. You're not a burden. I just think it's a bad idea to harbor things. If something is bothering you, then get it off your chest. As for Margaret, she's been through her own drama, as have I. She could probably tell you stories for days and offer you good advice. We're all coming from the right place and should be here as a support system for one another. It's what girlfriends do."

Frankie watched as Meg gazed out the window at the water. "I won't push it if you don't want me to."

Meg shook her head with a look of disgust consuming her face. "I just can't seem to get it right. Or at least, I haven't been up until now. But even that's about to change."

"Okayyy, that's a good start. But what exactly are you referring to?"

The server placed water on the table and explained the lunch specials for the day.

"I'll take the shrimp and grits, please," Frankie responded, settling on her favorite meal while Meg put in an order for grilled scallops.

Meg leaned in after he was gone. "I need to take several steps back and evaluate the head space that I'm in. Here I am on one of the most beautiful islands. I should be living it up. Basking in the beauty and celebrating that I've actually created the life I've always wanted to live."

"But?" Frankie asked.

"But – instead I find myself way out in left field, trying desperately to catch the ball, chasing it down with no such luck. I didn't get it right in New York before coming here. And, apparently, I'm still getting it wrong."

"Okay."

"Frankie, I didn't plan on meeting Parker, but when I did, I honestly started to have feelings for him. It was like he was some sort of prince charming or knight in shining armor, rescuing me at a time I needed it most. Of course, me being the idiot that I am, as soon as I felt sparks flying between us, I ran, uncertain if it was real or just me chasing after love."

Frankie tapped the table with her fingernail. "Negative. You're not an idiot for leaving. It was reasonable for him to expect that a single woman like yourself would want to seek out your own place to live. Right or wrong?"

"Right, but I ran immediately after the kiss, Frankie. He's not dumb. It probably shot his confidence way down."

Frankie rolled her eyes. "That's not for you to worry about. He's a grown man. He can handle his feelings. Besides, I suspect this isn't over yet. Mark my words, your knight in shining armor sounds like an intelligent guy. If he knows what's best for him, he'll come around," she grunted. "I like the guy, to be honest. He took you in when you needed help and he treated you like a queen. In my book, that's what you call a gentleman. But the idea that he might not be over his wife, that's the part I'd keep an eye on."

Meg fiddled with her napkin and sighed. "I guess we all come with one form of baggage or another. I certainly know I do."

Frankie flashed back to an image forever etched in her mind. It was from a video of her and her former groom waving to their guests on their wedding day. An experience from her mid-twenties she rarely spoke about. An annulment was all it took to dissolve the union. In six short months, the marriage was over and served as nothing but added weight to her baggage.

"Are you okay?" Meg asked.

She waved. "Oh, yeah. I'm fine. Just reminiscing, that's all. Trust me when I tell you, I have so much relationship baggage I probably need a U-Haul to carry mine around."

Meg laughed. "Frankie, please."

"It's true."

The feeling of a finger tap on the shoulder caused Frankie to jump. "Margaret!"

Towering above her was a model-like figure giving off an aroma that smelled like flowers.

"There you are. I was starting to think you weren't going to make it." Frankie stood with her arms open wide. "Come here and give me a hug. It's been way too long." Then she turned around. "Meg meet Margaret. Margaret, this is my wonderful housemate, Meg."

"Hi, it's so nice to meet you, Meg," Margaret said.

"Likewise. Here, we saved a seat for you. Make yourself comfortable."

Once Margaret settled in and placed her order, the conversation continued. "I hope I didn't interrupt something important. You two looked like you were in the middle of a pretty intense conversation. Poor Frankie darn near jumped out of her seat when I tapped her."

Meg raised a finger. "I'm to blame for that. I probably should've introduced myself by saying, my name is Meg Carter, and I have on-going, perpetual man troubles," she laughed. "That's actually an awful introduction, but it's what we were in the middle of discussing."

"Ooh, honey. You and I just became instant besties if that's the case. My middle name is man troubles. It's to the point where I've given up on dating," Margaret replied.

Frankie shook her head back and forth several times. "You two are something else. I knew you'd hit it off, but I refuse to allow us to sit here and have a pity party."

Margaret waved. "Oh, I'm not having a pity party. I'm long past that stage. I'm just stating a fact. I can't remember the last time I met a good man. Not back in the states or here on the island. At some point you have to call it like it is."

Frankie's eyelids closed. "Okay, I agree, but at what point do we stop blaming the men and take responsibility for ourselves? I mean, it's the same old sad, repetitive story every time. This guy has commitment issues, the other guy likes to string women along, and the other can't keep his zipper zipped long enough to save his life."

Meg sprayed water out of her mouth, quickly grabbing her napkin to dab the table. "I'm sorry," she snickered.

"You okay over there?" Frankie asked.

Meg nodded. "It was the zipper that did it for me. Keep talking, I'm listening."

Frankie transitioned her attention to the waiter as he laid down their tray. "Maybe we should ask this handsome fella his opinion."

Margaret and Meg watched intently.

"Sir, what advice would you give to single women who

want to find the right man and are tired of meeting Mr. Wrong? Maybe you can shed some light from a male's perspective," Frankie said, observing his nameplate that read James.

"I'm certainly no expert on these kinds of matters, ma'am. I've had three wives and I'm currently working on my fourth. Although, I truly believe the fourth time will be a charm. When I finally figure out the key to keeping a woman happy, I'll report back and let you know," he chuckled, placing the sizzling hot dishes on the table.

"Thank you, James. Best of luck to you and wife number four," Frankie smiled. That wasn't exactly the example she was going for, but she still wished James all the best.

When he left the table, Meg chimed in. "That leads me right back to the beginning of this conversation. I stated that I feel like I've been out in left field chasing something that always seems to elude me."

Frankie nodded. "Right, the ball chasing analogy. You can't seem to catch it. But, what does that have to do with failed relationships?"

"I'm glad you asked. Perhaps the relationships are failing because I keep chasing after something that's not meant to be chased."

Silence fell over the table.

Meg bowed her head momentarily, then picked up her fork. "I've been doing this whole thing wrong. Yes, I'm a hopeless romantic who wants nothing more than to find the right guy and fall in love. Who doesn't want that? But, pursuing it until it consumes you, or thinking that every guy you're attracted to may be *the one* is just downright foolish. That's not even what I was raised to believe. Why I ever allowed myself to go down this rabbit hole is beyond me."

"Interesting," Margaret replied.

Frankie's eyebrows crinkled. "So, you're blaming yourself for what your ex did to you?"

"Of course not. What John did was wrong. Period. But I made a choice to sacrifice three years of my life to be with an absolute jerk because I wanted the relationship to work. At some point, I think I wanted the relationship more than him. Sounds downright pathetic if you think about it."

Margaret patted her lips with a napkin. "I totally get what you're saying. I can recall the times when I knew the relationship wasn't right, and I still stayed for all the wrong reasons. It's like some sort of trap we fall into. We don't see anything better in sight, so we just stick with it because it's familiar."

Frankie laid her hand at the center of the table. "I'd buy into that if we're discussing our past. That's who we used to be. But what are we going to do differently to ensure that we never encounter these kinds of relationships again?" She looked around, then lowered her voice. "No offense to James, but I don't want to figure this thing out after four marriages."

Frankie bit into her succulent shrimp, recalling that she already had one failed marriage under her belt. She tried everything within the six-month stretch to be the perfect wife, hoping she'd convince him to stay. But it didn't matter. In his eyes they'd lost their chemistry, communication had become minimal at best, and the intimacy had dwindled down to an occasional shared meal over the five o'clock news. All excuses coming from a man who never really wanted to be married in the first place. Why he ever said *I do* was still a mystery to her to this day.

Meg laid her fork down. "It takes a lot more than four marriages for some people. Some take an entire lifetime to find true love. Some never find it at all. I just know that for me personally, the pursuit of love has to stop right now before things get out of hand."

"What do you mean?" Frankie asked.

"I want a fresh start. One that doesn't involve me worrying about when I'm going to find the right man. I refuse to drive myself crazy and be consumed with this kind of thinking anymore. I want out."

Margaret positioned herself to look directly at Meg. "And, if the right guy finds you instead? Then what are you going to do?"

A lazy smile emerged on Frankie's face. "Yeah, good point. Since you seem to have this whole thing figured out, what will you do then?"

"I can tell you what I won't do. I won't be so quick to accept an engagement ring from someone who's not worthy. I also won't allow another man to take me on a joy ride while he figures out what he wants to do with his life. My time is too precious to be wasted."

Frankie snapped her fingers twice. "You go, girl. Nobody's going to mess with Meg Carter," she laughed. Once the cackling among the three settled down, she continued. "Just promise me one thing."

Meg blew a piece of hair out of her face. "Margaret, why is your friend always giving me such a hard time?" she teased.

"Hey, for as long as I've known Frankie, if she's staying on me about something, she's usually right," Margaret confessed.

Frankie smirked. "Thank you, Margaret. Now, where was I? – Oh, I remember. I was going to make two simple requests. Not just of Meg, but of everyone, including myself."

Meg stabbed a fork into her last scallop. "Which is?"

"We agree to let the past go, completely. Take the lessons you've learned with you and allow the rest to become history. If you have to go as far as writing every hurt, and every wrong decision on a piece of paper, and then burning it in a fire pit, then so be it. Just let it go."

Margaret shook her head in agreement. "That's fair enough. What's the second request?"

Frankie picked up her glass and raised it before the women. "Remain open-minded about the future. I'm not suggesting you sit around and wait for Mr. Right. You both know how much I believe in going on adventures and taking each day as it comes. But, when, and if, he shows up, don't be so quick to turn him down because he's not this image of perfection that you've created in your mind."

Margaret reached for her glass. "I'm in. Lord knows my current plan isn't working," she chuckled.

Meg raised her glass. "I can toast to that as well. Of course, I'll have to begin with some soul searching and a lot of paper burning first."

The sound of clinking glasses rang in Frankie's ears, marking the day that she too would finally follow her own advice. The first day that she would make a decision to be free from past regrets and past heartaches.

Chapter 14

Parker

"Mom? Savannah didn't mention anything about you coming to visit. And, Ally, what's going on? How long have you two been here?"

Parker widened the door, allowing his mother, Evelyn, in and watching as Savannah crept in behind his middle sister, Allison. He always knew when Savannah was up to no good. This time was no exception.

"How long I've been here is irrelevant. A mother has a right to check on her son every now and again. Even if he's an adult."

He propped the broom against the wall and wrapped his arms around his mother, giving her a slow squeeze. "Of course, you do. Although usually I receive some sort of a heads up. This place has dust everywhere," he said, throwing a dagger Savannah's way, then playfully grabbing Allison. "Ally, you were in on this too, I see," he smiled.

Standing with her arms open she said, "hey, what can I tell you, Park? When momma bear hears that something's wrong with one of her cubs, she's catching the next flight out of

Chicago and there's nothing anyone can do about it. You know how she is."

Parker rubbed his forehead. "Okayyy. So, does anyone plan on telling me what's going on? I just spoke to dad the other day and he didn't mention a thing about this trip. It seems like I'm the only one in the dark here."

Seemingly ignoring him, his mother inspected the living area of the beach house. "Looks like you found yourself another nice place to renovate. The views driving up here were spectacular. Savannah, what was the name of that nature area again? The one we passed leading up to the house?"

"Lookout Point?"

Evelyn pointed. "Yes, that's it. It was simply breathtaking. The perfect spot for taking a lovely young lady on a date."

His eyes roamed over to Savannah, again throwing daggers, realizing it was very likely she'd been updating his mother on his love life, or lack thereof.

"Parker," his mother said, snapping him out of his eye war with Savannah.

He cleared his throat. "Yes, Mom?"

"Don't just stand there. I'd like a tour of the house. I want to see this work of art that's been consuming so much of your time as of late."

He lifted his hand, guiding her toward the kitchen. "Follow me. The majority of the credit for the kitchen remodel goes to Savannah. Her design ideas made a huge turnaround, making this one of the major focal points of the house. Marble countertops, a glass backsplash, beautiful tile, and a touchless faucet in the farm style sink."

Evelyn paused, marveling over the new chandelier, gliding her hand across the counter and taking it all in. "I love it!"

His sister Allison also toured the kitchen, admiring every nook and cranny. "When are you guys coming back to Chicago again? My house needs a bit of an uplift. It screams early-nineties and could use a little brotherly and sisterly love."

Savannah laughed. "I'll bet, but are you going to show your brother and sister some love in the form of cash?" she teased, holding her hand out for money.

"Alright, you two. Looks like there's a backyard retreat with my name on it. Let's head outside," Evelyn said, sliding open the newly replaced glass door.

Parker couldn't understand why he felt nervous, but he did. After all, he and his mother had always maintained a close-knit relationship. His parents had been with him through some of the best and toughest of times. They were there for all of his firsts. His high school and college graduation, the day he embarked upon his career, the day he met his first love, and the day she moved away and broke his heart.

Then there was Jenna. They were even there to welcome her as a new member of the family. And, they'd even been there to show their support at her funeral. They'd been there for everything. So, of all times-- why was he so nervous about his mother being there now? It didn't make sense.

Evelyn gasped. "Oh my stars. This is it. Somebody pass me a tropical beverage and a sarong. It feels like I've died and gone to heaven."

The sound of the ocean washed away Parker's anxiety, allowing him to let out a deep breath. "It is dreamy out here. I think it's going to make a perfect home for the right buyer."

His sisters wandered down to the lower level to sit by the pool. That's when Evelyn turned his way. "I was hoping you'd decide to become the right buyer."

He chuckled. "No, not this time, Mom. I haven't quite found the place that speaks to me yet. Don't you worry. I imagine I will someday."

"Hmm. I'm not so sure. You haven't found a place that

speaks to you since Jenna was alive. Seems to me like you need a wake-up call if you ask me."

He looked his mother in the eyes. "What do you mean?"

"How long has it been, Parker? Three... four years? You can't keep this charade up forever. Running from place to place and not planting roots is no way to live."

"I agree."

A look of surprise rested on his mother's face. "Oh. Well, that's good to hear. You should consider this house for yourself. You were able to buy it well below market value, and it's a perfect fit for someone who needs more stability in his life. I know losing Jenna hurt, but you can't keep running forever."

Parker leaned over the banister. "Again, I would have to agree. At least on the last part about Jenna. As for the house, I've already invested quite a bit to renovate and was looking forward to the return it would yield."

Evelyn leaned in beside him. "Son, some investments yield returns that are far more valuable than money. As a matter of fact, one of the greatest assets we possess is love. You can't take the rest of this stuff with you, but you can hold onto love forever."

Her words hovered over him like a storm cloud, weighing heavy on his mind.

"Now, rumor has it that you met and even lived with a very nice young lady for a period of time. One that you were very attracted to," she said in a blunt fashion.

In that moment it was as if he heard the sound of a mic drop in his mind. He suspected she'd come to dig into his business. At least his love interest or his inability to love after all these years. Either way, it was the very thing that made him nervous. They were close, but this was one subject he hadn't delved into as of late. Like a lot of moms, she had the ability to knock him right out of his comfort zone. And, he wasn't sure if he was ready for that yet.

"Sounds like Savannah has been keeping you informed," he suggested.

Evelyn shook her finger from left to right. "Savannah has nothing to do with this. What I was hoping to hear you say is you've learned a valuable lesson from your experience."

In Parker's opinion everyone always had such wonderful words of wisdom to impart. But somehow, he still never felt any wiser or any stronger after what he went through.

"What was I supposed to learn, Mom? I'd like to know. Sure, I was attracted to her. And, like someone who was so out of practice, I managed to overdo it and run her right out of this house. Epic fail if you ask me," he said.

The corner of Evelyn's mouth curled upward. "I know the whole story, Parker. Clearly you didn't do any harm if she came back to see you again. I'm not sure why you turned her away, or why you're always so critical of yourself. Jenna is gone. We will always have a special place for her in our hearts. Correction, while you will always have a special place for her in your heart, you have to give yourself permission to meet somebody new. She would've wanted that for you, Parker."

Moisture clouded his vision. "How do you know that, Mom? The cancer came back from remission taking her and our unborn child like a thief in the night. If only you knew the kind of guilt I carried for being so irresponsible."

"Irresponsible? How?" Evelyn asked.

Parker slapped the banister, then walked away. "I should've never entertained the idea of having a child. At the time she wanted it so badly, and so did I. We thought the worst was behind us, so how could I say no? But, in hindsight I was such a fool. I should've weighed the risk. We were so busy living off a false sense of hope!"

He'd finally said it out loud. The words that lingered in his mind, but he never vocalized. Not even in therapy.

Evelyn pulled up a lounge chair. "I see. So, to make sure I have this right, you think the passing of your unborn child is your fault?"

He nodded. "I could've done more to prevent the pregnancy from happening."

"But Parker, you're not God. You're not all knowing. You and Jenna were living your lives just as you were supposed to. If you suspected for one moment the doctor would come back with a six-month prognosis, you would've done differently. What a heavy burden to carry! Is that why you've been retreating from the world?"

He shrugged his shoulders. "I guess," he said, dragging a spare Adirondack chair beside her.

"Son, to the best of your knowledge, did the doctor give Jenna a clean bill of health?"

In a low baritone voice he responded, "Yes."

"Hmm. Well, I can't tell you what to do or how to feel. Lord knows I've carried my share of guilt over the years. But it has gotten me absolutely nowhere. In fact, I was always worse off because of the guilt and the shame that I carried. The one thing I know is true, the longer you hold onto guilt, the longer it will steal your joy and try to keep a firm grip on you to the extent that you can't live at all. Is that what you want for your future?"

"No, of course not," he said.

"Mm hmm. Exactly. Take it from me, Parker. I'm your mother, but I'm also a woman who's been through a heck of a lot. Including the loss of what would've been your younger brother or sister if I ever had the chance to carry the baby to full term."

Parker's eyes widened.

"Yes, that's right. I had a miscarriage right around the time you were getting ready to graduate from high school. And, believe me, back then, guilt and shame were my middle name. I questioned why I allowed myself to get pregnant at such a late age. I tormented myself with the *'If only this'* and *'If only that'* thinking maybe the baby would've made it if I had done differently--"

"It wasn't your fault!" he interrupted.

Evelyn clapped slowly at first, then began picking up the tempo.

"My point, exactly. Now, do you see where I'm going with this?"

Parker glanced over at his sisters who'd made their way further down to the beach. Easing into his chair he said, "I get it. And, Mom, I'm so sorry for your loss. I really am. But truthfully, I needed to hear this story. I'm so sick and tired of living my life alone. Deep down, all I really want is relief."

Evelyn laid the palm of her hand over his. "That's my boy. Or I guess I shouldn't say that, but you'll always be my boy."

They chuckled, allowing Parker to feel even more free. "You know, the woman that Savannah told you about. There's something about her that's special. In a lot of ways, she reminds me of Jenna."

"That's part of the reason why I came to visit. Outside of giving myself an excuse to take a vacation, I thought I could come out here and nudge you a little. Maybe push you in the direction of introducing me to your lady friend. You can only imagine how disappointed I was to hear you'd already given her a pink slip."

He smiled at the thought of Meg. "I didn't want her to go. I just didn't think I was worthy of her time. She's been through a few things herself. The last thing she needs in her life is another disappointment."

"Interesting. You know, Parker. In a lot of ways, you are just like your father. That's something he would do. Making assumptions about what I need and what I don't need. It drives me bananas. Although I know deep down inside, he means well. Don't you think your friend would like the opportunity to decide for herself if you are worthy of her time?"

He stretched his hands back, propping them behind his head. "I guess I never thought about it like that. I just know what I've been through and maybe—"

"Maybe you just take things one day at a time. See how it goes from there. Forget about trying to be perfect. Life just doesn't work that way."

Parker looked at his mother. "When did you get to be so wise?"

She fanned her hand toward him playfully. "You know what? I ought to –"

But before she could finish, Savannah popped her head around the corner. "Is the coast clear?" she smiled.

"Savannah Jeffries, you are officially in my doghouse," Parker teased. "You, Ally, and Mom planned this behind my back without saying a word."

Allison pumped her fists. "Yess, and we did it successfully. That's what family is for. I can't think of a better person to have an intervention with than with yours truly," she said, pointing to their mother. "Now, as for the rest of our time here, I want nothing but the Bahama breeze and a gorgeous tan before we go. Understood?"

"Yes, ma'am," he said, giving up his seat. "Not only that, but how about we plan to do something as a family while you're here? Maybe I can even take off a day or so."

Savannah raised her hand to her side. "Since when does Parker take off from work? Keep it up and I'll have to take your temperature to see if you're feeling alright."

"Ha ha, very funny!" he laughed.

Evelyn piped her voice up above everyone else. "Now, now children. We're just here for a few days, and I also plan to be a beach bum for the majority of that time. I just have one small request."

Everyone fell silent, leaving nothing but the sound of the crashing waves to fill the atmosphere.

"No pressure or anything, but maybe you want to introduce us to your new friend before we leave. You never know, she might –"

"Motherrrrr!" his voice escalated, leaving his sisters toppled over in laughter.

Chapter 15

Meg

"Dad, I'm fine, really. The job is great, my new living arrangement is working out for now. I couldn't be happier," Meg said, pacing around her home office with her video chat in hand.

"I'm glad you're fine, Meg. But Mariam and I would still like to come visit sometime and see for ourselves. We care about you," he chuckled. "And it doesn't hurt that you chose to live in a vacation hot spot, giving us even more reason for regular visits."

It hadn't dawned on Meg that anyone would make the effort. She always envisioned herself being the one packing and traveling home. Plus, she'd been so consumed since the day she landed, this was the first time she could consider these kinds of things.

"I'd love that. Ideally, it would be even better when I can provide a room for you to stay in. I'd hate for you guys to pay for a hotel."

"Meg, you are my daughter. I'd book a hotel on the moon

for you if I had to. Let's talk about it and make plans soon, okay?"

"Sounds good, Dad. I love you."

"Love you too."

Meg disconnected the line and made a beeline for her chair at the sound of the doorbell. Assuming it was just a courtesy ring from the delivery guy, she began skimming over emails, thinking nothing of it. It was his daily practice around noon to leave packages for Frankie who was a serial online shopper.

She had to admit, work from home days were way more productive as she wore jean shorts and a tank, and comfortably situated herself at her desk. With her favorite morning shows quietly playing in the background, she felt like she could think straight and accomplish most tasks by two in the afternoon.

Another ring from the doorbell grabbed her attention. "For the love of --" she sighed. "Who in the world could this be?"

Walking barefooted upstairs, she caught a glimpse of a man in uniform.

"May I help you?"

"Good afternoon, I have a delivery for a Ms. Meg Carter."

"I'm Meg Carter."

The delivery man looked back at his van. "I'm Sebastian, from Tropical Floral. I have a rather unique delivery waiting in the van for you, ma'am. If you wouldn't mind waiting here, I'll be right back."

Puzzled, Meg responded, "Okay. You sure you have the right Meg Carter? I haven't been living here that long."

"Ha! I'm certain of it, ma'am. As far as I know, you're the only Meg Carter living at this address," he yelled back.

Meg mumbled, "Good point."

She watched as he set up a rolling cart, stacking vases upon vases of flowers on top.

"Are you serious?" she whispered.

Sebastian rolled toward her with what appeared to be at least two-dozen pink roses. "As serious as a heart attack, ma'am! It looks as if somebody has an admirer."

Her eyes widened. "This has to be some sort of mistake."

"No mistakes here. Instead, I have specific instructions for you to follow. It's simple. Each vase is labeled with an envelope. They're all in sequential order, so please be sure to open the envelopes accordingly. If not, the boss will be upset with me."

Meg giggled. "We certainly wouldn't want that." Looking over the flowers once more, she then motioned toward the house. "I'll go grab your tip."

"It's not necessary. Everything is paid for. Where would you like for me to put your delivery?"

Meg looked around. "Um, would you mind bringing them inside? There's a table to your right as soon as you go in."

"Yes, ma'am."

She lifted a cellophane wrapped arrangement, gasping at their beauty. "My, my, these had to be expensive."

"They're certainly not the cheapest selection on the shelf. However, the cost is minimal if the person you purchase them for is of high value to you." Sebastian smiled.

After his last trip inside, he collapsed the cart. "I think that about wraps things up. Take care and enjoy your flowers."

"Thank you."

He waved and then yelled back to her over his shoulder, "Oh, and one more thing. Welcome to the Bahamas. It's a wonderful place to fall in love!"

"Uhm, thank youu--" her voice trailed off.

Inside, she inhaled the aroma of fresh cut flowers as she inspected each envelope. With curiosity eating away at her, she ripped open the first one, reading as follows, 'Meg, allow me to start by apologizing for the way things ended. It was never my intention for things to turn out the way they did." She rolled her eyes at the immediate disappointment of learning the flowers were from John. In some ways, maybe it was stupid of her to think otherwise. But of all people. *Ugh!*

She continued reading. 'I was heartbroken to learn that you'd left New York. Please don't be upset, but after jumping through many hoops, I was finally able to locate your forwarding address. I hope this delivery finds you well. If any part of our love still means something to you, please continue onto envelope number two."

The heat rising in her body was enough to make her perspire. With her teeth clenched it was all she could do to keep her cool.

Meg was clear she wanted nothing to do with accepting an apology from John, but she opened the second envelope simply because it was there. 'Words can't describe how much I messed up. I was wrong about everything. About us, about our future, even about my decision to walk away.'

She tore the note in half, tossing it on the table. *You've got to be kidding me!*

A male's voice cleared his throat. "Who's kidding you?" The voice chuckled, nearly startling her as he stood in the entrance of the door that was partially ajar.

Meg turned to see a smile quickly dissolving from Parker's face. He stood with a bouquet of his own in hand. "Parker. What are you doing here?"

The moment was awkward at best. Here she was standing in front of an arrangement from her ex. Something she couldn't even begin to explain if she tried. Not that she had to.

"Um..." He looked over at her flowers, and then down at his. "I was stopping by to surprise you. Really to apologize for being an idiot the other day," he said, pointing toward her delivery. "I guess my timing is off. It looks like you already have flowers of your own."

She glanced back at the arrangement that symbolized a weak apology, from a weak individual, arriving several days too late.

"Meg?"

"Yes," She looked up.

"It may be too late. Who knows? Maybe I've missed my opportunity." He took a step toward her. "Clearly, I'm not the only person who admires you. But if this is my chance to jump to the head of the line, then I'm taking my best shot."

Parker allowed his bouquet to fall to his side. "I want you. That's what I should've said to you the first time, but foolishly, I didn't. I want to learn everything about you. I want to smell the scent of your hair again and kiss you just like we did the first time." He hesitated. "I'm so sorry for turning you away like I did. That was just me running away from my fears."

Her heartbeat sounded like it was thumping loud enough to give all her secrets away. Truth was, she liked him too.

"You're not the only one with fears, Parker. One of my biggest fears is displayed right here on this table. This is the result of investing over three years of my life into someone who dropped me like a bad habit." She laughed, sarcastically. "Now he wants me back. Go figure. Guess things didn't work out with his —" She stopped mid-sentence, not allowing herself to convey what she was really thinking. "If this is what happens when you take a chance on love, then I'm good."

Again, he pointed to the flowers. "No. This is what happens when you encounter a selfish jerk. Big difference."

He moved in closer. "This is what happens when you encounter a real man, who's ready to explore love again. Someone you can actually trust with your heart." Her eyelids closed at the touch of his soft lips colliding rhythmically into hers.

"Oh, dear," she whispered.

Parker held back. "Do you want me to stop?"

"No. Not as long as you plan to be a man of your word."

She could feel the warmth of his breath drawing closer. Parker gently lifted her chin. "How about you allow me the opportunity to earn your love? To treat you the way a woman deserves to be treated," He offered, quietly. Then he dove in again, dropping the flowers to the floor.

She felt the strength of his arms holding her, the intensity, yet gentleness of his mouth pressed against hers. And the only response she wanted to give in return was another kiss.

* * *

The following morning, across from Meg's desk sat the regional director, her big boss and only boss located within the region. It was their first in-person visit, a bit odd from the previous hospitality culture she was immersed in. Although, in the current age of technology, it seemed like everything was virtual anyway.

"Ms. Chapman, it's such a pleasure to finally meet with you and enjoy a little face to face time," Meg said.

"Please, call me Linda. And yes, the pleasure is all mine. I'm always so busy traveling from one location to the next, or working from the home office. This certainly is a welcomed change. Meetings like these are among my favorites," she explained, fiddling with her thumbs.

"The team at The Cove have been raving about you, Meg. Before we continue with the agenda, I was wondering how you're settling in. Not only in your position, but on the island. I can imagine it must be quite an adjustment."

Meg's snort and hand wave probably exerted more energy than intended. "It's been an adjustment, alright."

"Is everything okay?"

She carefully reined in her thoughts, narrowing it down to a safe topic. "Well, in New York City there's no way I could wake up to a beach within walking distance. It's unheard of. The temptation to lay back and allow the sun to melt all my cares away is very real out here."

The look of concern eased as Linda smiled. "Yes, yes. Although we work in the resort industry, somehow the beach aspect never gets old. If only there was more time built into our schedules for r&r. How about your living situation?" she asked, while strategically tucking her hair behind her ears. Meg noticed it was about the fifth or sixth time she'd done it, along with adjusting her notepad and repositioning her materials several times. If this was the result of her being a workaholic, then the woman clearly needed a break.

"It's quaint. I'm renting with a friend for a little while until I settle on where I want to live."

"Smart move. It's so difficult planning these things from a distance. If you want, I'll have my assistant email a list of areas that might be a good fit."

Through the rumor mill, Meg heard she was a bit obsessive-compulsive over small details, a mega sales enthusiast, and made very little time for socializing or dating. Most of the staff attributed the lack of a man to her stiff personality. But, Meg on the other hand, didn't think the assessment was fair. After all, she didn't have a man and was nowhere near being compulsive or anti-social.

"Thanks, I'd appreciate it. In the meantime, I suppose you'd like to discuss my sales performance."

Linda slid on her glasses while flipping the page on her notepad. "I do have a few bullet points I'd like to cover. According to my records, you've already landed a golf tournament and a benefit event for the beginning of next year. Great job."

"Thank you."

"Mm hmm. However, as our regional sales director, that's the kind of volume we're expecting to see year-round. I'm looking forward to you picking up the pace. Think about how fun it would be to have round the clock events to close out the remainder of this year. I can see it now, even more weddings, fundraisers, concert series, you name it. Sky's the limit."

Meg wondered if she was hearing her correctly. She was on board for expanding her sales goals. Who wouldn't want to grow? It was one of the main reasons she accepted the job. But there was a way to go about it. And, converting The Cove, a five-star resort from a tropical relaxing getaway into a three-ring circus wasn't exactly the best way to go about it. It wasn't even the vision they painted to Meg during her interviews.

She winced. "Linda, of course, I'm willing to comply with whatever you wish. If there's a better way to do this, I'm on board and certainly open for ideas. I was just wondering if the additional traffic would cause our clients to leave negative reviews. Think about it. People come here to unwind. It's what The Cove is known for. If we ramp up the year-round volume to the extent that it becomes too busy around here, how is that any different from booking a hotel room in the middle of a major city?"

Linda looked up from her notes. "Oh, don't be silly. Even you admit that city life can't compare. Where would people go to the beach? I think we'll be just fine."

"Okayyy. Then what about our competition? Again, I'm happy to do whatever you ask of me, but don't you think year-round traffic might draw in unwanted traffic, therefore sending our clients to competing resorts? There are other ways to hit our sales goals without lessening our standard."

Again, Meg observed Linda one at a time, tucking her hair perfectly behind her ears. She suspected the woman had to develop a skin irritation at some point from all the pulling and tucking. *Good grief.*

"I thank you for the input. It's something I'll have to consider going forward. But, for now, I'd like to think I know what makes this resort tick." She leaned forward. "You see, Meg. During our interview selection, I was on the verge of choosing another candidate. But you said something during the last round that caught my attention. If I recall correctly, you had a goal of becoming the top sales director on the island within your two years. Is that correct?"

"Well, yes, but –"

"Exactly. And I too have a goal of hitting the top regional sales director. Except my deadline is by the first of the year. And since your performance impacts my performance, one would think it makes sense to be on the same page."

Meg swallowed. "Yes, ma'am."

Immediately, Linda's serious demeanor dissipated, and she returned right back to smiles and rearranging supplies. This time the rearranging was taking place in her briefcase rather than on her lap. Nevertheless, Meg was tempted to lean over from her desk to see just what the heck she was doing. Thankfully, she didn't because Linda popped up with a few papers in hand.

"Wonderful. Now that we're on the same page, I have a list of vendors and previous clients you might want to reach out to." She slid the list across the desk. "Oh, and here's another one I made of new clients I'd like for you to contact. Then finally, this third list is suggestions from a colleague. Take it or leave it. I'm not really impressed," she said with a fake smile.

"Uhh, okay, sure. I'll get right on it. Maybe I can even come up with a few ideas as well."

Linda let out a short breath. "Yes, do that. How about you gather your findings on a spreadsheet, and email it over to me within the week. That way we can keep an open line of communication and make sure we're on the same page."

Breathe and smile, Meg. Breatheee and smile, she thought to herself.

"No problem," she responded, quietly thinking if she were a drinker, now would've been a good time to indulge.

After closing the door behind Linda, Meg allowed her back to rest on the door, wishing she were in the comfort of her own home. Even better, wishing she was held captive in Parker's arms again. Something she hadn't yet shared with her best friend.

Meg grinned, placing her on speaker as she slid into her leather chair. "Case, are you busy?"

"Nope, just dropped the kiddos at their grandparents' house, and I'm taking a nice peaceful drive back into the city. Craig and I are having some mommy and daddy time this weekend."

"Niceee. What do you have planned?"

"I couldn't tell you. He took it upon himself to organize a romantic weekend for me. His only request was that I wear my new dress on Saturday night, and I requested that later on he wear his uniform," she chuckled.

"His uniform? What for? Wait, on second thought, I don't want to know."

"Ha! A good girl never kisses and tells, anyway. Now, enough about me. How's island life treating you?" Casey asked.

"Good for the most part. But it's like I'm in this weird space where if one thing is going well, then something else starts to fall apart. I don't know."

"Give me an example."

Meg glanced at the clock, noticing she was a few minutes into her lunch hour. "Do you want the good or the bad first?"

"Get the bad out of the way. That way we can end with the good," Casey replied, honking her horn in the background.

If it wasn't for Meg's meeting with her boss lingering in the back of her mind, it's possible she would have a different outlook.

"Let's see. Just had a meeting with my regional boss and in so many words she made it clear that she expects me to help her snag the title of lead Regional Sales Director by the beginning of the year. Way to spring that on me just weeks into the new job. She didn't mention specific consequences, but she certainly laid the pressure on real thick, making me feel like my job was on the line if I didn't perform."

"Yikes."

Meg groaned. "Yeah, she's basically asking me to achieve the impossible. At this point, her goals are so unrealistic, it's laughable. The only problem -- she's not joking."

"She sounds like a piece of work."

"She's a nightmare, alright. I won't even get into her perfectionist tendencies, or what the others are saying about her. I just know she's definitely going to be a handful to say the least."

"Sorry, Meg. I know that has to be frustrating."

"It is," she sighed, easing down into her chair with thoughts of Parker and the previous night. "And, then there's the good news."

On the other end of the line Meg could hear Casey's windshield wipers swooshing back and forth. She took a moment to soak in her view of a blue sky, with traces of white clouds and endless ocean water for miles and miles. One of the best office views she's ever had.

Casey egged her on. "Come out with it already. Is it about your former roomie, the sexy beach house dude?"

"Case, you're so crazy. His name is Parker, remember? You

of all people should know because you encouraged me to investigate the guy," she smiled.

"So, it is about him. What happened? Did he ask you on a date?"

She closed her eyes tight, biting her lip to prevent from squealing. "As a matter of fact, I did receive a text on the way to work, this morning, asking me on a date. But, that's just the icing on the cake. Everything really began with a kiss yesterday. Case?"

"Yes."

"I don't know what it is about him, but his kisses are electrifying. And his touch... the way he holds me. Then there's his vulnerability. It's like we've both been through so much, but we're still drawn to taking these small steps of faith, hoping it will lead to something bigger. It's crazy."

"Well, well, well. Listen to you. Is this the same Meg who proclaimed to have guard rails up, wanting to protect herself from the world?"

Meg nodded. "I know. I know. I figured you'd remind me of that. Look, Case, navigating this new chapter of my life hasn't been easy. I never had the chance to tell you, but after we last spoke, I took your advice and worked up the courage to go over and talk to him."

"Obviously it went well," Casey said.

Meg considered it for a moment. "Things actually didn't go according to plan that evening. But for some reason, he was compelled to personally knock on my door, with flowers in hand, and apologize. That has to mean something. Look, I don't know what's to come of it. Maybe nothing at all. But in the name of remaining open like you and Frankie asked me to do, I'm going on the date."

Casey shouted from the top of her lungs. "Whoo hoooo.

John, wherever you are, I just want you to know that my girl Meg is moving on, leaving your sorry behind in the dust, baby!"

Meg held her chest, trying to contain her laughter. "Oh my goodness, Case. You're too much. If you think that's something, then wait till you hear this. I almost forgot to tell you about John's flower delivery. Probably because I've already dismissed it in my mind."

"Stop it. He sent you flowers? What for?" she asked.

"I couldn't tell you. I stopped reading after opening card number two."

Casey gasped. "There were more?"

"Mm hmm. Eight to be precise. A long-drawn-out way to beg for my forgiveness after realizing he made a mistake. Those were his words, not mine. I suppose he thought sending an elaborate arrangement would impress me, somehow. I don't get it."

"Unbelievable," Casey replied.

"Yep. Parker arrived shortly after I read the second envelope, taking my mind off the whole thing. By the end of the evening, I threw every bit of it away, getting rid of it the same way he got rid of me."

If Meg was being honest with herself, there were probably warning signs in the last year that she chose to ignore. Like the infamous way he always took phone calls in another room. Or the way he kept his cell phone locked at all times, requiring a code to get in. She never wanted to be that woman who pressed her man about every little thing. All she wanted was a relationship based on total trust.

"Meg, this has been one heck of a year for you, kiddo. But I'm proud of you for hanging in there."

A hissing sound escaped as Meg exhaled. "Thanks, Case. Now if only I can figure out a way to top Linda's sales from last year. I doubt I'll have a life, but if I can pull it off, at least I can hold on to my job."

"Don't worry. With your track record, you'll navigate that too."

Again, on the line Meg could hear horn blowing, signaling her to look at the clock. She was down to thirty minutes left on her break.

"Well, it sounds like you're getting close to the city, and I've yet to run out and grab something for lunch. Can we catch up soon so we can give each other updates?"

"Absolutely, my friend. But, Meg, before you go, I have something I want to tell you."

Meg reached for the lower drawer in her desk to grab her purse. "What's up?"

"I'm pregnant. Craig and I are expecting twins."

"Shut up!! No way, are you serious?" Meg asked.

"Yes. It's still early, but you know I couldn't hold something like this from you."

"Aww, Case. Congratulations. You must be so excited."

"Uhh, excited and nervous at the same time. Our house is already crazy, so you can only imagine what will happen when we come home with twins."

"Oh, but it will be so fun having newborn babies again," Meg smiled.

Casey chuckled. "I'm glad you feel that way. Be sure to remember this conversation when we need you to fly in and lend a helping hand."

"You know I'd be there in a heartbeat, friend."

Chapter 16

Parker

"So, this is the infamous Parker I've heard so much about. My name is Frankie. It's nice to meet you," she said, extending her hand.

Parker felt her giving him the once over. He was okay with it, knowing that girlfriends usually had to give their official stamp of approval.

"Hi there, Frankie. It's nice to meet you as well."

"Meg will be upstairs in a moment. You can come in if you'd like."

"Thanks, but it's such a nice evening. I don't mind waiting on the porch if it's okay with you."

"Sure, make yourself comfortable. I'll go let Meg know that you're here."

Parker took a seat on the front steps, recalling the last time he'd taken a first date seriously. He could distinctly remember what he planned for the date, what he wore, and how he felt like a ball of nerves. This evening felt no different, other than the apple of his eye was Meg this time.

The sound of heels approaching made him perk up.

"I hope I'm not overdressed," Meg said, pushing her way out of the screened door.

He felt frozen, trying to rationalize how he'd been so lucky to meet Meg. Was it a coincidence that one man could discover someone who'd captivated his heart, not once, but twice in a lifetime? He didn't think so. It had to be something bigger than happenstance.

Frankie peered her head around Meg's shoulders. "You two have a wonderful evening."

He returned the well wishes, never once taking his eyes off Meg.

"Thank you. You do the same," he replied.

Meg spun around. "How do I look?"

"Amazing, to the point where I'm having a hard time focusing on anything else."

"Seriously? Because I didn't know if the dress would be too much or –"

Parker reached his hand out. "Shh. I wouldn't lie to you. You look stunning. Come. Follow me. I promised to show you a good time tonight and it's time to deliver. Are you ready?"

He was certain his heartbeat was racing at an abnormal rate. It was the effect of walking beside the woman who did things to him that he couldn't explain. The mere touch of her warm hand in his was enough to give him an adrenaline rush. Something he hadn't experienced in God knew how long.

"Parker."

He paused before reaching the car door. "Yes?"

"I just want to clear one thing up with you before we go out tonight. It's something that's been lingering ever since you stopped by and — I figured if it's bothering me, then it might've crossed your mind too."

He smiled. "The only thing on my mind is getting past the

point of feeling nervous around you. It may seem childish, but you make me feel like a teenager in love."

Meg released her hand from his, gently gliding it along his cheek.

"There's nothing childish about that. The way I see it, we're both chartering upon new territory here. We're both curious, excited, yet —"

He interrupted. "Cautious?"

"Exactly. But no matter what, there's no reason to be nervous. Let's just enjoy one another and see where things go from here."

This time Parker took a step closer, cupping her cheeks between his hands. "It's a healthy kind of nervous. A good feeling on the inside that I'm willing to explore. Now, tell me. What's been on your mind?"

"I was waiting for you to ask me more about the flowers yesterday. But you never said a word. Weren't you curious to know who they were from?" she asked, speaking softly.

With their lips now inches apart, he knew the electricity between them could easily give way to a kiss. But he intentionally stayed the course, saving the tender moment for later. "The way I calculate things is simple. Someone may have sent you flowers, but I was there, in person, taking a risk of being rejected to ask you on a date. Since you accepted, I think that has to count for something, don't you?"

Meg snickered. "Yeah, I guess since you put it that way."

When his heart rate slowed down to a somewhat normal pace, Parker opened the door to his truck.

"Good. But since you brought it up — should I be worried? Is there someone else out there vying for your affection?"

"No one worth talking about. But, for the sake of being transparent, it's just my scumbag of an ex who had a revelation that he made a big mistake. Unfortunately for him, I'm not impressed. I guess he thinks I'm supposed to feel sorry for him and come running back. No, thank you! Again, no one worth talking about!" she expressed.

"Well, lucky for me then. Since that's behind us, what do you say we get outta here? I know a place where we can dine and dance until the sun comes up if you want to."

"Ooh. He's a dancer. My kind of guy."

He stared at the woman standing in front of him, recognizing this was more than a first date. Instead, this was a fresh start with his potential forever love.

He lowered his voice as he traced two fingers along her temple. "Interesting. I was just thinking you're my kind of woman."

The more time Parker spent with Meg, the more he felt at ease, and even at one with her. The laughter, the way she glided on the dance floor, the childhood stories... all of it combined, giving him an adrenaline rush like he'd never experienced before.

"Meg," he said, swaying slowly and off rhythm to the upbeat tempo in the background.

"Yes?"

"Full disclosure. The first day at the house, when I discovered you standing out on the deck –"

"Yeah," she whispered, hanging on every word.

"Within minutes I knew there was something different about you."

She covered her mouth, partially concealing her smile. "There was something different about me all right. I was putting up a lot of opposition, demanding that you didn't belong at the house. When in actuality, I was the one who didn't belong there."

Parker nodded. "That may be the case, but I never wanted you to leave. It actually hurt when I discovered that you'd left," he admitted, then continued. "I don't know if you've ever experienced a situation that you couldn't explain or make sense of, but you just knew in your heart it was right. That's kind of what was happening to me while we were at the beach house together."

Meg listened as he spun her around, completely dancing to the beat of their own drum. "I've also had situations that felt right in the beginning, but ended up terribly wrong for me. How do you know the difference between the two?" she asked.

"Personally, the mere fact that I tried to run when I recognized I had feelings for you. Ha! That was my first indicator. Plus, I was fortunate to sit under the wise teaching of a lady who happens to know me very well. She had a good kick in the pants conversation with me, helping me to see the error of my ways."

Meg chuckled. "Was it your sister?"

Parker's face turned red. "No. I probably should be embarrassed to admit this, but the wise lady is my mother. She's in town visiting, and let's just say she's the only one with enough chutzpah to tell me when I'm acting like a fool. You don't have to worry, though. I'm not a Momma's boy. She just knows how hard the journey was to get to this point, and I guess she didn't want me to miss out on another opportunity."

"Opportunity?" Meg asked.

"Yes, an opportunity to pursue a really good woman," he paused. "An opportunity to pursue you."

"Well, I like your mother already. I probably need to talk to her myself, because I too was ready to give up on love. Sometimes we all need a good old-fashioned kick in the pants. Something to help get us back on our feet again. Wouldn't you agree?"

Parker agreed, but found himself distracted, not only by her beauty, but by the erratic fluttering in his stomach. The only thing he could think of to help ease the stirring was to lean in and give her a soft, yet steady kiss. One that she readily received.

* * *

Parker eased on the brakes, while turning down the road leading to Frankie's place. Every ounce of him wanted to spend more time with her, but ultimately, he knew it was best to get her home at a decent hour.

"I had a great time with you tonight," he said, easing his hand over hers.

The corner of Meg's mouth raised slightly. "I had a great time with you as well."

"Maybe we could –" A lump formed in his throat as he slowed down in front of the house. He tried to speak but couldn't find the words as he stared past Meg, looking out the window.

"Are you okay?" she asked.

He lifted his finger, pointing at a man sitting on the porch, buried in a sea of flowers. "It looks like you have company."

He'd give anything for his assumption to be wrong. However, the only thing Meg managed to do was exhale, sitting motionless, while staring out the window.

Meg cleared her throat. "I don't know why he's here."

"Well, it's obvious he wants to talk with you. Maybe you should go hear what he has to say," he said, easing his hand off hers.

She turned to face him. "Parker, you have to know that he's

here uninvited. I would never accept an invitation to go out with you only to turn around and —"

"You don't have to explain yourself, Meg. I'm good," he said, opening the palm of his hand. "Take my hand for a moment, please."

He waited as Meg slid her hand in his, then folded his hand over hers, giving her a gentle squeeze. "I'm not going to lie. This guy is completely ruining my plans to end this night with an amazing, Fourth of July fireworks kind of kiss." The two laughed in unison, then he continued. "But, I think it's important that you go ahead and speak with him. If you want to talk tomorrow, you know where you can find me."

"Are you sure?" she asked.

"I'm certain."

Chapter 17

Meg

U*nbelievable. What is he doing here? What... is... he... doing here?*

As if thinking it repeatedly would make the situation go away. Meg wasn't delusional. She hadn't fallen and hit her head. John, the same guy who she'd once been engaged to. The man who'd left her for someone else was now sitting in front of dozens of roses, arranged meticulously leading up to the door.

Had Frankie seen this? she wondered, trying her best to settle her mind from the ongoing barrage of thoughts. She stopped, closed her eyes, and took a deep breath, then watched as he rose to his feet.

"John."

"I know what you're probably thinking, Meg. Let me explain."

"You... have... no idea what kind of thoughts are running through my mind. No idea."

He signaled her to stop. "I know, but let me at least try and take a stab at it. You're probably wondering why I'm here, and why I flew all the way from New York to be here and—"

"And, what makes you think showing up on my doorstep is going to influence me one way or another?"

He cautiously held his hands out. "Hadn't exactly considered that. But I was thinking that sending flowers wasn't enough. That's the sort of thing you do on birthdays. This occasion calls for me to be here."

Meg raised one hand to her hip, noticing the windows were dark in the house, making her assume Frankie was out.

"So, you play stalker online and God knows where else to find out where I live. And, once you succeeded in finding me, you think spending hundreds of dollars in flowers is supposed to win me back over. Is that how it works in your mind?"

"Meg, no. That's not what I was trying to do. Did you read all of the notes?"

She slowly shook her head, feeling her temperature rising with every word uttered out of his mouth.

He continued. "I'm sick, Meg. My test came back with high PSA levels. The doctors say it's my prostate."

Meg felt frozen in time as if everything around her had come to a complete stop. The sound of the trees swaying was nonexistent. The evening breeze was non-existent. Even the adrenaline rush from wanting to deck him in the face had left her body, leaving her feeling numb.

"Is this in the advanced stages or --?"

"Doc seems to think surgery should turn things around. It may leave me with some side effects that I may have to deal with. But nothing's guaranteed. Only additional testing and keeping a close eye on things post-surgery will tell."

"So—you're not dying?" she asked, squinting her eyes.

"Well, not as far as I know, but this whole thing is scary as heck. Undergoing surgery with no one to be there by your side is a lot if you ask me. My folks are too busy chasing major financial acquisitions in the UK to have time for me. I couldn't think of anyone else to reach out to but you. Plus, I miss you, Meg."

His words hit like a sucker punch, sucking the wind out of her gut.

"Mm," she grunted.

"Everything I wrote in the letters was true. I made the biggest mistake, foolishly chasing after someone else when I should've remained with you. I admit my faults, Meg. I was wrong. All of this was explained in the letters along with the diagnosis. And, when I didn't receive a call from you the night of the delivery, as I begged you to do in the last letter, I thought the only thing left to do was catch the next flight, just to come out here and prove my love for you. Now, I'm here," he said, holding his hand against his chest as if he were some sort of hero.

There was no such thing as keeping her cool, or even trying for another second to be somewhat understanding. He'd lost his mind. Literally, he'd lost every last one of his marbles. **And, it was time that she told him so.**

"Let me guess. Your new boo was too busy for you as well, leaving you with no choice but to call little old Meg. Is that how it happened?"

He stuttered, "No – not at all. We broke things off about a month ago."

"And, in a month's time, precisely when your results came back, is when you decided you needed me back in your life? Is that the correct version?"

She watched as he paced, seemingly trying to get his story together. "What's the matter? Cat gotcha tongue?"

He sighed. "Come on, Meg. Don't do this. Of all the people in my life, you were always the one who really cared. Even when I didn't deserve it."

"John, the hole you're digging keeps getting deeper and deeper. If I were you, I'd choose my words very wisely. And, for the record, when I was there, you decided you didn't want me anymore. Remember? You dropped everything we had together like a bad habit. Although, I can't say that I'm upset about it at all."

The more she thought about it, Meg had always been the giver in the relationship, but not as fortunate when it came to receiving. Financially, he had everything. Therefore, he used his money and his influence to get what he wanted. But the very thing she needed most was his heart and his love. Something he was incapable of giving.

He cleared his throat. "What are you trying to say?"

Meg's back stiffened like a board. "I'm sorry about your test results. I'm even sorry to hear that you will need surgery. I wouldn't wish any of these things upon anyone, not even my worst enemy. But the good news is, it sounds like there's hope for you, John. Something that most wish they could say." She bowed her head, finding it difficult to make steady eye contact.

"What about us? I meant it when I said that I miss you, Meg. When you've been with somebody for almost four years, that love doesn't just go away."

Meg rolled her tongue along the inner portions of her mouth, trying her best not to unleash the foul thoughts running through her mind. Instead, she walked the remaining steps bringing her within three feet of his frame. Placing her hand directly over her heart, she said, "The love I had for you doesn't live here anymore. Anytime one finds themselves with a selfish individual such as yourself, the relationship is destined to fail. It's only a matter of time. And John, that's exactly what happened with us. I gave and gave and gave of myself unselfishly. You, on the other hand, depleted me, leaving me broken." She dusted her hands off. "And now, I'm done. As in --

really done. The only advice I can give you at this point is to go find your girlfriend and beg for her forgiveness."

She walked past him, hoisting her dress slightly as she climbed the front steps. That's when this feeling like a weight had been lifted washed over her.

Meg turned around. "It's too bad you didn't call me, John. I could've saved you the flight money. But, now that you're here. Thank you. I didn't realize how much I needed this." She then proceeded to grab her keys. "Oh, and if you wouldn't mind doing me a favor. My roommate will probably be coming home shortly. Would you be so kind as to clean up the mess before she gets back?" She pointed to the flowers. "I'd hate for her to have to step over everything."

"Uh, yeah. Sure."

The sight of his disappointment did nothing for Meg. Not even spark an ounce of regret, but instead relief that he was out of her life. And this time it was for good.

Chapter 18

Casey

Almost three months into her pregnancy, Casey had yet to experience the typical signs of an expecting mother. No nausea, no dry heaving, no strange cravings, except for her newfound obsession with pickles. Overall, she was feeling good, which prompted her to book a flight and pull up a beach chair alongside Meg and Frankie for some quality girl time.

"Ladies, thank you for inviting me for an impromptu visit. I needed this more than you know," she said, lathering her legs with sunscreen.

With the hot sun beaming down, their bodies glistened as if they were advertising for a fifties swimsuit edition. Each of them fashionably sported a suit that displayed tummy control or high waisted bikinis, as if they really needed it.

Casey continued. "Before you know it, I'll be so far along in the pregnancy I won't be able to fly anywhere, so I might as well enjoy it while I can."

Meg smiled. "How did Craig feel about having the kids on his own for the week?"

"He was just fine, the minute he found out nana and poppa were coming to lend a helping hand," she chuckled. "Men are so funny. If it were me staying with the kids everything would continue along as usual. Between camp and swimming lessons, plus weekend activities I'd see to it that they had plenty to do. When Craig takes over, all of a sudden, we need to call for reinforcements. It's hilarious."

Frankie nodded. "Hey, whatever it takes to ensure you get a break, that's what matters most."

"I couldn't agree more," Casey agreed. Then she acknowledged Meg. "Now that I'm here, I can totally see why you chose to make this your new home. The island is gorgeous. Just heavenly. I'd relocate here in a heartbeat if my life wasn't already established in New York City."

Meg agreed. If she were being honest, there were parts of her that missed the city as well. But she could always visit, satisfying her desire, while still maintaining her new lifestyle that included much more tranquility. "If you ever decide to uproot yourselves, I'd figure out a way to help make it happen. I'm sure Frankie could tell you the same. We know of families here that are from other parts of the world. And they have little kids just like you. Nothing's impossible, Case."

"I know. But for now, Craig has his career, and the kids absolutely love being close to their nana and poppa. I couldn't imagine us living our lives any other way. At least not for now. You, on the other hand, have really turned a new leaf." She waved her hands around.

"Yes, but I still have a ways to go. Frankie has been gracious to let me stay with her for as long as needed. But I'm starting to get the itch to get out there and find a place to call my own. Then, there's my job. My boss certainly is surprisingly —"

"Unreasonable," Frankie chimed in.

"Yep, that's probably an understatement, but we'll go with it for now," Meg nodded.

Casey propped her beach chair upright. "Okay, so we have a little work to do. Maybe a few areas to tweak. But for the most part, I'd still say the life you're living now is way better than how things were when you left. Do you remember your last month in the city? You were waiting on pins and needles to hear about the job, and you wanted nothing more than to get as far away as possible from your memories with John."

Frankie interjected. "Oh, not that guy again. Please, don't get me started on John. I've never even met him but even I know that he's a piece of work. Did she tell you about what he did a few weeks ago? Showing up at my doorstep like some sort of desperate loser who doesn't know how to take no for an answer!"

Meg rolled her eyes. "Good grief. Of all topics to discuss. I'd much rather decide where we're going for dinner tonight, wouldn't you?"

"Not so fast. You didn't mention anything to me about John coming here," Casey said, lifting the brim of her hat.

"That's because I didn't think it was worth mentioning. I saw him for what — maybe fifteen minutes, if that."

"And?"

"And he tried to buy his way back into my life. It was an unexpected move, but I didn't fall for it. I let him know under no circumstances was I coming back. That's it. End of story."

Frankie shot upright, positioned to protest. "That's not the end of the story. Tell her about how he tried to recruit you to be his nurse's aid. I'll bet Casey will really get a kick out of that!"

Casey watched Meg draw in a long breath. She knew her friend well enough to tell she was past the whole matter and ready to move on. But she needed to hear the details for herself. After all, she'd been around through the years, watching Meg pretending to be happy with John, but always knew she could do better. Way better!

"John did mention something about needing surgery and having no one to be there for him. He said his PSI levels were high. But he also confirmed that he wasn't dying, so that in itself gave me some sense of relief. When I asked him whether his new lady friend could help take care of him, he told me they'd broken up," Meg said, sliding her sunglasses on.

Casey took a moment to process everything, then she said, "So, wait a minute. You mean to tell me he flew all the way out here to half get you back and mostly recruit a private nurse for his surgery?"

"Yep, that's it in a nutshell. But are you surprised, Case? I sure as heck wasn't. He'd already sent flowers prior to and gone through all the motions. It's his typical attitude that basically thinks if he tosses around enough money, he can have his way. Who cares? I'm so over it."

Casey let out a chuckle. "Well, alrighty then. If you're over it, so am I. The only thing I want to know at this point is when do I get to meet your new beau?"

Frankie relaxed back in her chair, kicking up her feet. "You mean her new boo," she smirked.

"Frankie, did I ever mention how bad you are at this? There should be a gentle introduction and flow to this sensitive kind of topic. You can't just blurt everything out," Meg said, somewhat chastising and mostly teasing.

"Mm hmm. I'll have to keep that in mind, but for now if you'll slowly turn your head toward the three o'clock hour, you'll notice your future husband walking this way," Frankie said.

Casey immediately glanced to the right, allowing Meg to be the subtle one if she wanted to. Not that looks were everything.

Heck, John was good looking and still turned out to be a first-class jerk.

"Meg, I remember you saying he was cute, but according to my calculations, cute doesn't even come close to describing this yummy hunk of a man," she said.

While holding her smile in place with her teeth locked together, Meg managed to mumble, "Will you two quit, please!"

She'd quit all right. For now, at least. But Casey wasn't going to rest until she had a chance to meet Meg's new man. This way she could see for herself what he was really made of.

Chapter 19

Meg

Her heart couldn't beat any faster than it was in that moment. Parker was treading through the sand, looking particularly handsome while toting large paper bags in hand. And, her best friend was sitting beside her, waiting to meet him. Ready to give her honest feedback. She wouldn't want it any other way, but still thought the moment warranted a little warning. "Parker was nearby for a meeting and offered to bring us snacks. Casey, you know I love you dearly but –"

Her friend stopped her mid-sentence. "I know, I know. Use my God given filter and save all my thoughts for after he leaves. Got it," she winked.

"Right." But before she could say another word, Parker's shadow began hovering over. He wore khakis, a polo shirt, and looked just as scrumptious as he always did. The best part was he never seemed to know it, or at least he didn't care.

"Good afternoon, ladies," he said.

"Any man who comes bearing lots of food to a woman

who's expecting is already a keeper in my book," Casey chuckled.

Frankie waved. "I'm not pregnant but I love to eat, so I'm with her. What do you have there, Parker?"

Meg couldn't help but laugh, noticing there was little room for the unfamiliar with those two. Casey had always been transparent with anyone she'd met, but she'd come to learn that Frankie was just as much of an open book. It was something they shared in common.

Parker placed the food down on their chairs as they sat up. Then winking at her directly he said, "I know this was supposed to be a snack, but if there's any way to win the hearts of Meg's good friends, then I'll do whatever it takes. In this bag you have traditional all-American burgers with all the fixings. And, just in case you were in the mood for some local delicacies, this paper bag is filled with all the flavors of the island. If it were me, I'd start with the last one for sure."

Frankie spoke up. "By any chance do you have a brother? If you do, I'd be happy to meet him sometime. I'm just saying."

That was all it took for the whole group to break out in laughter.

* * *

After indulging in a full-blown meal, smiles, and a lot of not-so-small talk, Meg managed to steal away for a moment to stroll along the shore with Parker. She stopped to face him, holding his hand. "Thank you for doing this. The food was amazing. You really outdid yourself. I think the girls were impressed."

"It was my pleasure. Trust me, I knew coming here that your friends would have a lot of questions about me. I wanted them to have a chance to see for themselves that I'm genuine and put to rest any concerns they may have."

"Concerns?"

"Yes," he said, stopping to embrace her by the shoulders. "I may be in the early stages of getting to know them, but it doesn't take much to realize they want what's best for you. They love you and just want to ensure that I'm nothing like your ex. And that's fair."

He ran a single finger down her arm, sending a current through the pit of her stomach.

"I think they can already tell just by the way I talk about you. You're different, Parker."

"That's right. I am different. I've been through enough heartache and pain to do everything I can to avoid it at all cost. I would never intentionally inflict pain on you," he said, gently tracing his finger across her heart. "Do you believe me?" He leaned in, holding her steady as their eyes met.

"Yes. But I'm sure it was that way with Jenna as well. You guys couldn't help that she got sick. You would've never done anything to hurt her and I'm sure if she were here, she'd offer you the same level of commitment. You loved each other and that's very different from what took place between John and me."

Parker looked away. "That's true, but there's something you need to know. Something I've told very few people, but if we're going to be together, you need to know all of me."

Meg clenched, hoping this wouldn't be the moment where he'd admit something that would disappoint her. She'd already had enough disappointment to last her a lifetime.

"Okay," she replied.

Parker began explaining. "Once the cancer went into remission, and the doctor gave us the clearance to get back to living our normal lives, I was so excited to have all of it behind us, I kind of threw caution to the wind."

He remained silent, seemingly searching for the right words.

"It was probably selfish of me, but I just wanted to enjoy my wife, never considering what kind of consequences could come along with her getting pregnant."

He continued strolling slowly, allowing his feet to be overtaken by the occasional wave. "We were so excited when we got the news. And just when it seemed like life was giving us something to look forward to, the cancer came back. This time with a vengeance, not even allowing Jenna enough time to carry the pregnancy to full term," he explained.

Meg gasped, feeling like the wind had been knocked out of her. The experience itself must've been terrible, but the thought of carrying that kind of burden after all these years was even more heartbreaking. "Parker, you can't blame yourself for what you didn't know."

Parker turned, looking her in the eyes. "I've come to terms with it now. But, it's still a part of my past and I can't ignore my feelings about it. I still wish I had enough discernment back then to do differently. It's probably the very reason I've been living my life somewhat on the go. Always extra cautious, not allowing enough time to get too familiar with one place or with one particular person. At least not anyone except for the locals in passing. But all that changed when I met you."

A lazy smile emerged on Meg's face. "Really? Explain. What exactly does this change look like in Parker's world?" she teased.

"Well, the new and improved Parker wants to find a quaint cottage in the area to call home."

She nestled closer as he spoke. "Mm hmm. Continue. Tell me more about this new and improved Parker."

"Okay, well, the new and improved Parker was captivated the first time he laid eyes on the beautiful Meg Carter. It was something about the way she laid her foot down, claiming the beach house as her own that ignited a fire in him. Except, the one thing he never expected was that the fire would last. To this day, he's still sad that she packed her bags and left."

Meg wore a smirk across her face. "You never told me you were sad."

"I was. I wanted you to stay so badly. I would've given anything to experience one more day seeing you wake up with messy hair, or cooking with you, and staying up until all hours of the night talking over photos. I miss those things so much. I miss you."

She never experienced the kind of love that made one feel weak in the knees. But today was her day. If he didn't hurry up and take her completely into his arms, she was afraid her wobbly legs might give way.

"Outside of the messy hair, I miss those things too. But, we're here now. That's what matters most, right?"

"Right," he said.

"And, ever since I stepped foot on the island, I can admit you've been the best thing that's ever happened to me."

He caressed her in his arms. "Even better than your dream job?"

"Uh, the jury is still out on the job, but yes. Even better than my position at the resort. Meeting you was an unexpected but very much welcomed surprise," she explained.

"And what about John?"

"What about him? I presume he caught a one-way flight back to New York, deciding to never speak to me again. I'm at peace with it, given that all he was ever really about was his own selfish gain."

Parker gently kneaded his hands across her back. "So, if he's completely out of the picture, does that mean I get to be completely in?"

She leaned over, giving him a peck on the lips. "I thought you'd never ask."

Meg's view of Parker as he lifted her slightly above his shoulders, twirling her around was a sight she'd remember forever. But the real unforgettable moment was the way he gently placed her back down and surrendered to her sweet kiss.

Ready to head to the beach for book two? Click here to continue following Meg's journey in Tropical Escape!

New Tropical Breeze Series!

Can she find love when she's healing from heartache?

After a painful end to a long engagement, all Meg wants out of life is a fresh start.

She can't think of a better way to begin than by advancing her career in the hotel industry. When an opportunity comes along to accept a position at a five-star resort, she secures a beach house, packs her bags, and heads to the Bahamas.

But her oasis has been sold in an auction and the new owner and heartthrob, Parker Wilson, has no intention of holding onto a contract.

She'll have nowhere to stay, nowhere to heal, nowhere to grow if she gives in to his flippant attitude about her future.

When Meg digs her heels in and refuses to leave, will this drive them further into the arena of enemies? Or will they find common ground and potentially become lovers?

Tropical Encounter is a clean beach read with a splash of romance that's sure to give you all the feels.

Pull up your favorite beach chair and watch as Meg and Parker's story unfolds!

Tropical Breeze Series:

Tropical Encounter: Book 1
Tropical Escape: Book 2
Tropical Moonlight: Book 3
Tropical Summers: Book 4
Tropical Brides: Book 5

Solomons Island Series

She's single, out of a job, and has a week to decide what to do with her life.

He lost his fiancé to a fatal accident while serving in the coast guard.

Will a chance encounter lead Clara and Mike to find love?

Clara's boss, Joan Russell, was a wealthy owner of a beachfront mansion, who recently passed away. Joan's estranged family members have stepped in, eager to collect their inheritance and dismiss Clara of her duties.

With the clock winding down, will Clara find a job and make a new life for herself on Solomons Island? Will a chance encounter with Mike lead her to meet the man of her dreams? Or will Clara have to do the unthinkable and return home to a family who barely cares for her existence?

This women's divorce fiction book will definitely leave you wanting more! If you love women's fiction and clean romance, this series is for you. Embark on a journey of new beginnings and pick up your copy today!

Pelican Beach Series

She's recently divorced. He's a widower. Will a chance encounter lead to true love?

If you like sweet romance about second chances then you'll love The Inn At Pelican Beach!

At the Inn, life is filled with the unexpected. Payton is left to pick up the pieces after her divorce is finalized. Seeking a fresh start, she returns to her home town in Pelican Beach.

Determined to move on with her life, she finds herself

caught up in the family business at The Inn. It may not be her passion, but anything is better than what her broken marriage had to offer. Payton doesn't wallow in her sorrows long before her opportunity at a second chance shows up. Is there room in her heart to love again? She'll soon find out!

In this first book of the Pelican Beach series, passion, renewed strength, and even a little sibling rivalry are just a few of the emotions that come to mind.

Visit The Inn and walk hand in hand with Payton as she heals and seeks to restore true love.

Get your copy of this clean romantic beach read today!

Pelican Beach Series:

The Inn at Pelican Beach: Book 1
Sunsets at Pelican Beach: Book 2
A Pelican Beach Affair: Book 3
Christmas at Pelican Beach: Book 4
Sunrise At Pelican Beach: Book 5

Made in United States
North Haven, CT
21 November 2022